the
irony
of fate

a novel

Scarlett Adaire

www.scarlettadaire.com
Book Cover Design by ebooklaunch.com
Author Photo by Kelli Boyd
Interior Format
© KILLION
THE GROUP INC.

For Annie.
May your spirit continue to inspire us.

"Man plans. God laughs."
-*Yiddish Proverb*

CHAPTER ONE

Liz

LIZ STARED HARD into the bathroom mirror, try-ing to find any resemblance of the woman she used to perceive as herself. Sure, the reflection of the petite figure with long brunette curls and bright blue eyes looked familiar, but it was the soul behind the eyes that she didn't recognize.

"What have you done?" she muttered to herself in guilt. Closing her eyes tightly, her mind shifted to *him*. It had been six months since the first time they made love. Their initial encounter had been innocent on Liz's behalf. She'd had no intention of what proceeded to transpire. Their meeting over happy hour cocktails had been muddled with mindless small talk as they stumbled through their agenda, both distracted by the attraction that was generating between them. Their eyes were soft, but focused intently on each other, as if no one else was in the room. One drink led to three, and soon they were both too tipsy to make any sound decisions. As he walked her to her car, the awkward silence was as loud as a New York City street.

"Thank you for the drinks. I think I had one too many though," she giggled nervously. But as she reached to open her car door, he beat her to it.

"Liz, I should call you a cab," he commanded, perform-ing the gentlemanly gesture. His assertiveness took her breath away.

There he was, within inches, staring into her eyes, his firm chest covered in a slim fit button-down business shirt. As she looked up at him, there was no denying her desire. His large hands grabbed her face and slid back into her long, dark hair. Pulling her in close, the most delicious lips she had ever tasted were on hers as she felt herself melt into him. Like two teenagers recklessly ignoring all rules and inhibitions, they soon found themselves in her backseat, unbuttoning and unzipping every stitch of clothing in record time. Liz's legs were wrapped tightly around him as his lips kissed every inch of her they could find. The warning sirens blaring in the back of her head weren't loud enough to make her stop what was unfolding. She felt him slide deep inside her and neither could help but gasp at how amazing the sensation was.

"Liz, you feel even better than I imagined," he whispered breathlessly in her ear, sending a chill down her spine that sent her heart racing even faster toward destruction. It wasn't long before they were both grabbing and clawing, trying to get as close and as deep inside one another as humanly possible. Heavy breathing steamed up the windows, but it wasn't enough to hide them from the rest of the world. She had crossed the line, one she never dreamed she would trample over. But in that moment, she didn't care. They looked passionately into each other's eyes and paused, silently acknowledging their nervous leap into each other's soul.

He was, and would forever be, her Favorite Mistake.

"Liz? What in the world is taking you so long in here?"

Like a lightning bolt, Liz was zapped back into the present as her best friend, Cassie, slung open the door to the ladies' room. Music from the band billowed into the small, tiled space as chatter from the wedding guests roared in the distance.

"Sarah and I have been looking all over for you. We thought you fell in." Cassie laughed a tipsy laugh, but Liz knew Cassie sensed her awkwardness.

"Oh, I'm sorry, Cas. I got a little emotional. You know, weddings. They always make you think back to your own. I went a little overboard reminiscing about mine and John's wedding day. It's probably the alcohol making me so sentimental," Liz nervously justified to her fellow bridesmaid. Faking a smile, she grabbed Cassie by the arm, thwarting any further interrogation, pulling her back into the enchanted bubble of wedding reception bliss. She hoped her rationalization was convincing enough for Cassie. The last thing she needed was a suspicious, prying best friend to chastise her infidelity. She had enough of her own guilt to stifle.

"Let's find that hot bartender and get another round of those yummy concoctions he whipped up for us," Liz yelled over her shoulder as the two women held hands, weaving through the crowd of guests. They spotted the bride waving them over to the bar. Cassie seemed satisfied with Liz's ability to emotionally rally back into celebration mode and for that, Liz was relieved.

"Geez. Where have you been?" The new Mrs. Lutz held up her shot glass and impatiently slid two more down the bar to the previously-missing-in-action bridesmaids.

Clink. The ever so sweet sound of celebration. The three best friends beamed as they toasted the evening, tipping back shot glasses and indulging in liquid caramel heaven.

"To Sarah," boasted Liz. "May your marriage be as fulfilling as a Bradley Cooper movie, your favorite vibrator, and chocolate chip ice cream on a Sunday afternoon." Cassie and Sarah laughed and shook their heads at the per-usual cynical and inappropriate toast from the petite brunette.

"Yes, here's to Mrs. Hal Lutz." Cassie smiled endearingly at Sarah, leaning over to kiss her cheek. Sweet Sarah. The giving one. She had the patience and heart of Mother Teresa. She was destined to be the pediatrician out of their physician posse. Adorned in her ivory one-shouldered—goddess style—draped bridal gown, she was Athena on Earth that evening.

"You guys are the best." Sarah grabbed both of them, kissing their cheeks in maternal grandeur. "I can't believe this evening is finally here. Did I seriously just get married?" Sarah shook her head in disbelief as the three late-thirty-something, polished, and professional women squealed and giggled, jumping up and down like teenage girls that had just spotted Bieber.

"Girls, I'm sure this is the beginning of a chain reaction of good things to come for all of us." Sarah smiled compassionately, directing an unintentional glance toward Cassie.

"Yeah, Cas, you know they say it happens when you least expect it. You and Rick are here in this romantic place with plenty of time on your hands," Liz proclaimed sarcastically while throwing out a sexy wink and hip sashay. "Who knows, maybe you're already knocked up." Obviously not believing her own statement nor caring for the potentially unborn, Liz motioned for the bartender, catching a glimpse of Sarah and Cassie's locked eyes as they acknowledged each other's observation of her apathy.

"I'm pretty sure that's a negative, Ghost Rider," Cassie replied matter-of-factly. "Let's not bring this up right now. Today is Sarah's big day." Cassie raised her arms and gave her best Vanna White pose to frame the open-aired cabana-style St. Lucia venue. "Besides, you all know that I have my cycle down to a science thanks to all of the gazillion fertility apps out there right now. And I'm supposedly fertile starting tomorrow, so Rick gets no action until my fertility app alarm says he can." Cassie snapped her fingers in true diva style. The three women tried not to look suspicious as the topic of their conversation approached them.

By Cassie's account, Rick had been fairly nonchalant about the whole family planning process over the past few years. She had on multiple occasions expressed resentment that the stress of it hadn't seemed to faze her husband. "A typical man for you...completely detached and self-absorbed. I bet he's loving all of this extra action he's getting. Of course, Rick and his super-size ego are one hundred percent certain that his soldiers can get the job done. But me and my underproductive, dysfunctional ovaries ain't so certain, ladies," Cassie had admitted to Liz and Sarah.

Liz watched in envy as Rick approached his wife like a prowling lion moving toward his prey. She didn't understand how Cassie could ever muster the strength to turn him down, even if it was to preserve her strict conception agenda. It certainly wouldn't be difficult getting in the mood to make love to him. He was beautiful with his tall, fit frame and perfectly chiseled jaw line. There wasn't a woman in the world who would turn their cheek to him, not even Liz.

"Mrs. Lutz." Rick nodded and bowed, acknowledging the new bride. "Why are you ladies empty-handed? We need to take care of that." He motioned to the Lucian bartender, unaware of the minute time lapse since the trio's last round. He then changed his attention to his wife, pressing up behind her, wrapping his arm around her waist and planting a provocative kiss on the back of her neck. Liz heard Sarah snicker beside her. He was bound to get nowhere with his efforts up against Cassie's uncompromising objective.

"Mr. Buchanon, are you trying to get me drunk?" Cassie accused as she playfully unraveled from his grasp. "I'm certain that you're not trying to sabotage our fertility schedule. Must I remind you that we have to save your swimmers for tomorrow? It's game time and I need you

to be fully loaded." Rick grunted in defeat and playfully smacked her backside while Sarah rolled her eyes at
Rick's crude display of affection.

The air was knocked out of Liz's chest as she tried to
hide her jealousy. She quickly changed the subject,
attempting to regain her internal composure. "On that
note, where are those drinks you suggested?" Liz inquired.
The prompt return of the handsome bartender carrying
three freshly-filled shot glasses was a much welcomed
distraction from her covetous thoughts. "What's this shot
called by the way?"

The tanned and glistening provider of the liquid
heaven answered, "A buttery nipple."

"Well now, that sounds appropriate," Rick boasted.
"I will leave you ladies and your nipples to yourselves,
per my wife's request." Cassie gave him a sweet kiss on
the lips and a reassuring squeeze of the hand. The three
women watched as Rick moseyed onto the dance floor
with his proverbial tail tucked between his legs.

"I hate turning down that gorgeous man of mine, but
he will get his fill soon enough. I have to stick to my
guns, girls," Cassie chuckled, flashing her best *Charlie's
Angels* double pistol. Laughter thankfully broke the awkward air of the baby-making conversation. No sooner
had the second round of buttery nipples hit the back of
their throats, Sarah had Liz and Cassie by the hands, pulling them onto the dance floor. Liz's heart sank deep into
her chest as the all-too-familiar scene brought her back
to when their friendship began nearly twenty years ago.

———————

Eighty-nine nervous bodies gathered in the auditorium. Some lame professor was lecturing on and on
about how the next four years would be the best and
worst of their lives. Liz looked around at the unfamiliar
faces, disappointed and thinking for certain she was the

most normal of anyone in the room.

"Mom, it's horrible. I'm surrounded by complete nerds. It looked like an ant farming convention in there," she'd cried over the phone on her lunch break. But to her surprise, the bar at the class social that evening provided the perfect spot for finding some classmates with similarities. Liz, miserable and desperate for a drink, bellied up to the bar next to two other seemingly-miserable females, waiting on their complimentary drinks as any normal, poor students would do.

"Thirsty, ladies?" came a surprisingly charismatic voice from behind her. "I would offer to buy you drinks, but it's an open bar. Can I at least have the pleasure of ordering for you?" he asked in gentlemanly character. Liz and the charismatic blond made immediate eye contact. Instantly, she changed her mind about wanting to drop out of medical school. He was gorgeous with his wavy, surfer hair and just enough of a tan left from summer to highlight his bright green eyes and perfectly white teeth. Liz vaguely remembered noticing him in the auditorium that morning in orientation. He was by far the best eye candy in the geek-filled room.

"Ugh, I hate open bars. Terrible house liquors and wines, and we all know this is adding to our ridiculously high tuition. I'm Liz, by the way," she said, extending her hand toward the blond hottie for a proper introduction.

"John Hamilton. Nice to meet you. I assume you ladies all know each other already," he stated, smiling at Liz and the two women to her right. Liz was so distracted by John's appearance that she almost forgot she was amidst other company.

"No, we haven't been introduced yet," replied the bubbly, wavy-haired blonde. "I'm Cassie Campbell. Nice to meet you, John." They all three turned to the shy, petite blonde awaiting her introduction. Liz couldn't help but instantly notice her warm eyes.

"Sarah. Sarah Lowe," she replied softly, but with a sense of self-confidence. *This girl could be fun with a few drinks in her, I bet*, Liz thought to herself.

"Now that we've all been formally introduced, I propose a toast to Emory Medical School's class of 2005," John cheered as he distributed the subpar drinks that had finally been served. They toasted in unison, drinking to their futures, oblivious to how entangled their lives would become.

"Have you guys heard about the new club that opened downtown? I was hoping to break in their dance floor tonight. Something tells me that we're not going to find too many compadres here to join us." Liz scanned the room at the stern-faced gunners with their intentions set on being top of their class.

"I agree," John replied with a smug grin. "Looks like a bunch of damn Tarzans to me. They might as well beat their chests and swing from some branches." The four of them laughed at the ironic truth to John's analysis. It was confirmed that they were way cooler than the rest of the people in the room and so decided to ditch the scene and head into downtown Atlanta to Cosmopolitan.

Cosmo's was where their friendship story all began. It was eerily similar to this evening with the four of them drinking and dancing—besides the perfect St. Lucia venue, of course, and a few more wrinkles on their faces and dollar bills in their wallets. But their friendship had been tainted. There was no way to hit the reset button. And Liz didn't know if she would do that even if she could.

CHAPTER TWO

Cassie

A S IF ON cue, the handsome, green eyed blond made his way onto the dance floor, unable to resist the three ladies making moves without their escort. After all, John was the original patriarch of their clique. Cassie watched in awe as John locked eyes with his wife. She had always been envious of his unwavering commitment to Liz. Even in med school, Cassie had yearned for the same from her then-boyfriend, Dylan. What she would have given for that kind of devotion from him.

Cassie's heart sank. She missed Dylan at times like this, all of them together and celebrating. Who was she kidding? She missed him constantly. Her mind had been plagued for months with thoughts of how maybe Rick wasn't the one she was supposed to be with. She couldn't help but wonder if her infertility issues stemmed from a deeper place... a place of regret and what-ifs for her first love. *It's just the stress of it all. You love your husband.* But deep down, Cassie knew her frequent dreams of the past were more than fertility hormones playing tricks on her. Cassie hadn't had the courage to tell her two best friends about her recurring doubts. Just the unwarranted thoughts themselves were enough to cast extreme guilt into her soul, much less actually saying the words out loud.

Cassie smiled endearingly at her friends as John planted a passionate, reassuring kiss on his wife's lips and then leaned in to Sarah, scooping her off her feet, swinging her around like a ballerina.

"Johnny boy, you still have my heart after all these years," Sarah said endearingly to her old friend. The bride blushed as they continued to dance to the reggae beat, laughing and twirling around the dance floor. John was a great dancer. Liz and Cassie followed suit, grabbing hands and proceeding into their classic pretzel moves that always made an appearance after a few drinks and music.

"Okay, Liz, I'll lead and you'll follow." Cassie commanded as she twisted Liz around, spinning her behind her back.

"But of course, dear," Liz replied in a proper debutante tone, the two of them fully aware of Sarah's friends and family looking on, mostly with smiles and approval, outside of a few prudish-looking aunts that probably needed to have the cobwebs knocked out of their panties. Per usual, the dancing doctor duo overlooked the naysayers, and homed in on their own little American Bandstand routine.

"Liz, how's your triathlon training going?" Cassie yelled over the blaring reggae music, trying to switch her thoughts away from Dylan.

"It's going okay. I'm a terrible swimmer, so I'm super nervous about the half mile swim," Liz admitted half-heartedly while twirling under Cassie's raised arm.

Cassie's eyes widened at Liz's lack of confidence, seeing as she had never witnessed her best friend have a defeatist thought in her life, especially in regard to fitness. Liz was a modern-day Jane Fonda. She had practically competed in every half and full marathon in the nation. Cassie was baffled that a sprint triathlon would intimidate her, and her furrowed eyebrows gave away her thoughts.

"I know, I know. It's *sooo* hard to believe Mrs. Tough Exercise Lady is nervous about it." Liz shrugged. "Thank goodness I enlisted the skills and knowledge of your

amazingly athletic husband to help me with the training. He's competed in so many triathlons, I couldn't *not*
utilize his experience. I don't know what I would have
done without Rick's help the past few months."

"Oh, of course. Rick has seemed to really enjoy helping
you. He is kind of a hard ass, though. I hope he isn't being
too tough on you. He tried training me a few times and
I could only envision him as some sort of deranged drill
sergeant with veins popping out of his temples. I would
have sworn his baseball cap was hiding horns. You're handling his intensity better than I did."

"He's harmless. And besides, I needed a hard ass." Liz
reached around and cupped Cassie's right butt cheek,
giving it a firm squeeze.

"Liz!" Cassie squealed as they both broke into laughter at the thought of those crotchety aunts watching
and judging them. Rick swayed up to the two of them,
embracing them both with his massive wingspan.

"Getting frisky with my wife again, Liz?" Rick raised
an eyebrow and looked at Liz sternly.

"Oh, Rick, I had her first," Liz defended as she hugged
Cassie tightly, playfully giving Rick the stiff arm to back
away.

"Am I going to have to break you two ladies up again?
This is getting exhausting after all these years." It was
John, who had also come to claim his wife. The song had
ended, and Sarah had pranced off to find her new husband and finish her rounds greeting family and friends.

"May I cut in?" John bowed to Cassie as he took Liz's
hand, leading his wife onto the dance floor.

Cassie felt Rick's strong arms pull her in close. Taking
her hand, he spun her around to the new slow beat that
was playing. She could faintly hear the rhythm of the
ocean in the background. She placed her hands on his
strong shoulders and gazed up into his deep-set eyes. She
had always been a sucker for real men. You know, hard

jaw lines, strong brows, and pronounced cheekbones.You could do a lineup of all her past lovers and there were only minute details of difference between them. As she stared up at her husband, her heart ached with guilt at her earlier doubts. *How can you even think for a second that this man isn't the one for you?* She stroked the hard angle of his jaw while her thumb grazed the newly erupted bristles on his chin, despite their earlier trim. Rick leaned down and, with the only soft part of his face, planted a sweet, gentle kiss on Cassie's lips. As he pulled her in even closer, he nestled the nape of her neck, sending a warm sensation streaming through her core.

"Damn it," she whispered breathlessly. "You sure know how to push the limits." She was instantly reminded of what made her fall in love with him in the first place: her undeniable physical attraction to him.

Rick pressed himself firmly into her. "I'm a sucker for you in a tight-ass dress," he muttered, caressing her. "And those long legs that go for miles." He held his wife back at arm's distance, admiring his prize and gazing at every inch of her body from foot to hair.

Cassie blushed at the compliments, even if they were coming from her husband. "I definitely should have cut you off from the bar," she giggled. "And myself too. I'm not near as much of a baby-crazed stickler at this point in the night. You may get lucky after all, Mr. Buchanon." Cassie flashed a sexy grin and proceeded to pull him in close enough that their dancing neighbors didn't notice her hand stroke him.

Grabbing her hand, Rick pulled Cassie through the crowd to the cabana ballroom entrance. Reaching the edge of the boardwalk, they laughed as they haphazardly kicked their dress shoes into the air. The coolness of the sand between her toes felt like heaven on Cassie's tired, day-long-high-heeled feet. They were both a little unsteady as they trampled through the sand toward the crashing water. The warm air blew Cassie's blonde hair back. It felt so refreshing as it cooled her skin from the heat of dancing. She turned to see Rick's shirt pressed up against his perfectly sculpted chest from the same gust of wind. The foamy bubbles from the crashing waves reached her toes and she was thankful for her short dress. Rick wasn't that fortunate.

"Babe. Your pants." Cassie bent down to roll them up, but much to her surprise, he grasped the sides of her head, cupping under her jaw and pulling her toward him.

"Don't worry about me. Let's worry about you," he directed as he slid his hand under the turquoise cotton of her dress. "Commando, eh? I knew it. I was wondering how you would fit anything else underneath there." His attention shifted and Cassie could see him eyeing something in the distance. "Come on," he said with childlike excitement. She couldn't help but indulge in his escapade.

The moon was a surprisingly good beacon of light as Rick led them down the beach past the resort. Cassie could see where they were headed from its illumination. She had noticed the jetties earlier on a walk down the beach.

"Here. This is perfect," he pronounced, sweeping his wife up in his arms and gently laying her down on a large flat cool rock.

"What in the world are you doing?" Cassie barely muttered before feeling her legs separate and Rick's warm breath between them as he kissed her inner thigh. *I guess this commando thing could be convenient*, she thought, gazing up into the night sky. Cassie watched as the clouds moved quickly over the moon that shone huge behind them. It was the most beautifully erotic view. Hoping the sound of the waves would drown out any noise, Cassie loudly sighed a sweet sound of ecstasy as he arrived at his intended target. Breathing in deeply, she sucked in all the fresh beach air her lungs could possibly hold. All her senses were filled as her core tensed and her skin tingled with the ultimate pleasure. Touch, sight, smell, sound, and finally, the taste of her husband's kiss. "Your turn," Cassie slid her hand into Rick's slacks intending to return the favor.

Rick chuckled and pulled her hand away. "Now, now. I'm not going to let you regret this in the morning, Dr. Buchanon. This one is on me. Like you said, I need to save my swimmers for tomorrow."

"But that's not fair," Cassie pouted, reaching for his belt buckle once more.

"It's okay, babe. I can stand one night of just pleasing my wife," he reassured, pulling Cassie to her feet. "Now, let's get back to the party."

Cassie obliged, but before she walked away from the blissful moment, she paused, taking one last look up into the night sky. Her eyes caught a glimpse of a shooting star. Smiling, she made a wish for her very own happy ever after, made up of white picket fences, swaddled babies, and playdates.

Making their way back toward the reception, Cassie admired the blue and green paper lanterns hanging over the dance floor that skipped haphazardly like popcorn to the rhythm of the wind coming off the ocean. The candle-lit hurricanes on the high-top tables guided them like beacons back to their destination. Cassie spotted her two best friends on the dance floor and panicked, realizing the two of them must be wondering where she had disappeared to. "I'm sure Sarah and Liz are wondering where I am. I doubt I'll be able to convince them that this was a bathroom break," Cassie snorted as they trampled through the sand giving way beneath their feet. She straightened her dress and gave Rick a quick once-over, making sure they were presentable and hadn't left incriminating evidence on their attire. Thankfully, all those in attendance were several drinks in and unlikely to notice any disarray.

"There you two are." Sarah spotted them first as they made their way through the entrance.

"Just thought we'd take a quick romantic beach stroll before you guys got me so drunk that I couldn't walk." Cassie winked at Sarah, giving her the sign to not push the subject any further.

ding, ding, ding. The music had stopped, and Hal had taken over the stage with a few taps of a spoon on his crystal glass. He was made for Sarah. He was handsome, in a little brother kind of way, with his fit but smaller stature and his soft face and eyes. There wasn't an unkind bone in his body. As Cassie watched him proudly gaze at Sarah, she could just picture their new life together, volunteering on Saturday mornings at the local food bank and driving their Volkswagen with two golden retrievers in the backseat. The perfect little American couple.

As he began to speak, the final bits of chatter fell to silence. "Thank you, everyone, for coming so far to celebrate this amazing day with Sarah and me. Come here, dear." As Hal motioned his new bride to the stage, her face beamed at his words of endearment and she double stepped it to his side.

"I'm really proud of her," Liz whispered to Cassie. "Having the patience to wait for her Mr. Right."

"Yeah. Me too." Cassie smiled, understanding the weight of Liz's words as she thought back through Sarah's dating history. Sarah had never really dated that much in medical school, despite being asked out by many. Her focus had always been school, and her friends, of course. This had been so different from both Liz—who always had John by her side—and Cassie—who, despite being a class year behind him, spent any and all free time with Dylan.

Cassie's mind was torn from the past as Hal finished his

speech. It was time for Liz to enter her favorite place: the spotlight. Cassie hated speaking in front of large groups, so Liz had agreed to present the bridesmaid toast, even though Sarah had made it abundantly clear that they were co-bridesmaids, refusing to choose one over the other as matron of honor.

"You're going up here with me," Liz commanded, grabbing Cassie's hand.

"The hell I am. We had a deal," Cassie hissed, snatching her hand back. Her face instantly turned red as she felt the heat of nervousness rising on her skin.

Clenching her jaw in agitation, Liz stepped on stage and up to the microphone. She still looked stunning despite a shimmer of sweat and tussled hair from the evening's dance party.

"Good evening, everyone. I am Liz, one of the beautiful bride's best friends from medical school. I'm aware I agreed to give this toast alone, but it is only fitting that we also invite the other part of our trio to the stage. Please welcome Cassie Buchanon." Liz winked as she spoke into the microphone, clapping her hands together. The tipsy crowd followed suit, cheering for the tall blonde to approach the stage. Cassie would now have no choice but to abide by Liz's deceitful request with a few hundred guests smiling and urging her onto the stage.

Are you fucking kidding me? I just got laid down on a rock by my husband. There's no telling how I look. Incriminating for sure. I probably have moss stains on the back of my dress. I am going to kill you, Liz. Cassie reluctantly made her way to the stage, feeling the burning stare of those same judgmental aunts of Sarah's. Cassie cast an evil eye at Liz as she stepped toward her, one foot at a time. Cassie was as pissed as a hornet.

"Don't worry," Liz whispered to her as Cassie took to her side. "You don't have to talk. Just stand up here with me."

As Liz delivered the speech, Cassie took the advice of so many public speaking teachers. *Okay, find someone in the audience that you know and focus on them. Pretend like they're the only one there watching you.* Sarah and Hal were easy targets as they sat at the side of the stage, smiling, cuddled up in true newlywed fashion. Cassie's mind wandered off. *I wonder if they will try getting pregnant right away. As much as I love her, my heart will break if she gets pregnant before me. Ugh, I am such a terrible friend.* Cassie felt guilty for even thinking such selfish thoughts, but she couldn't help her yearning desire to be a mom. Liz and John already had two beautiful blond boys, Paul and Sam. The thought of being the barren friend crippled her. A family was all she had ever wanted. Three boys to be exact. But after two years of failed attempts, she was becoming less picky. *I will be happy giving birth to just about anything at this point, boy or girl. Hell, I'd even go for a giraffe, for Pete's sake.* Cassie's fears of the stage settled while her anxiety over life exploded. Her attention was abruptly pulled back to Liz as she raised her champagne glass and her voice several decibels into the microphone.

"….so, here's to Mr. and Mrs. Lutz. May all your dreams and wishes come true. We love you both." Liz turned to Cassie, flashing a coy smile, tipping her champagne glass to her best friend, begging for forgiveness. Cassie's overly firm tap of the crystal stemware let Liz know she hadn't quite forgiven her yet.

"Good thing I love you, missy." Cassie's eyes blazed at Liz before turning to find her husband waiting at the edge of the stage for his turn to toast the new couple with his wife.

"I couldn't tell if you were that nervous or if you were just really needing to go to the bathroom, your knees were shaking so badly," Rick chuckled, extending a hand to his wife, helping her from the stage.

"It was probably a little of both. Now move it, mister.

I need a bathroom." Cassie wove her way through the crowd, back to the small powder room she had found Liz hunkered down in just a short time ago. She hadn't thought much about Liz's odd behavior until she was reminded of it with her déjà vu-inducing abrupt entrance into the tiny bathroom. But this time, as she flung open the door, she was greeted by one of Sarah's aunts, who slapped her with a disapproving glare.

"Are you enjoying the evening, ma'am? Lovely, don't you think?" Cassie decided to speak and take the high road, pulling respectful etiquette from her Southern roots.

"Yes, dear."

Well, I guess that's better than "You're a slut," Cassie thought to herself. She immediately made her way to the full-length mirror, turning to check her backside, praying there was no incriminating jettie-rendezvous evidence caked on her dress. *Whew, all clear. Thank goodness.*

As she made her way back to the bar, she spotted Rick and Liz arm in arm, smiling and laughing. She was so thankful her friends had finally accepted Rick into their tight-knit group. He had worked hard to conquer Sarah and Liz. "Babe, what can I do to make them like me? I feel like I'm in the Spanish Inquisition every time we hang out. They give me a harder time than your father," Rick had pleaded on more than one occasion.

John had been easy for Rick to win over, considering their mutual love of sports and fishing, but the girls had thought he was a player. "I don't know, Cassie. Something just doesn't settle right in my gut about him. I can't put my finger on it," Sarah had admitted. Several years had passed and the girls had appeared to stifle their hesitation about Rick. And with Rick getting promoted to a new position in Tampa where John and Liz lived, it had been easy for the two couples to build a great friendship. As a matter of fact, they were practically inseparable. The only missing pieces were Hal and Sarah. Liz and Cassie both prayed that somehow Hal and Sarah would be able move to Tampa, too, but with both of them being physicians at Memorial Hospital in Savannah, they were locked into that city. So, for the time being, their friendships were built on weekend road trips and FaceTime girls' nights.

"You have to trust me," Cassie overheard Rick whisper to Liz as she moseyed up behind them unnoticed. Tapping him playfully on the shoulder, Cassie chuckled as he jumped being startled by her presence. "Oh, hey, babe. Liz and I were just discussing the game plan for tomorrow's triathlon training. Liz isn't liking what I'm expecting of her," Rick scoffed as Cassie saw Liz's face drop.

"Darling, please remember that Liz will probably be a little hungover in the morning, not to mention we're all on vacation. So, would you please take it easy on her? I'm not so sure about the healthcare situation on this island. I mean, we don't even have cell phone service."

"Cassie, do you think a triathlon is easy? This is the perfect situation for her to learn to overcome obstacles. She has to learn to push through pain and fatigue or she will drown in the lake." Rick argued.

"Now I understand your earlier reference to a drill sergeant, Cas," Liz confirmed.

"Like I said, *trust me*," Rick said firmly, staring intently at Liz. Liz's eyes lowered uncomfortably to her champagne flute.

"You'll be fine. Don't be nervous. You got this," Cassie reassured her best friend, kissing her on the cheek. "I'm so ready for bed. That stunt you pulled a few minutes ago on stage gave me a major case of fight-or-flight and now I'm crashing. It's been a long day, and it sounds like tomorrow will be even longer for you," Cassie taunted her best friend. Rick nodded in agreement as they both hugged Liz goodnight before seeking out the bride and groom to congratulate them one last time for the evening.

As Rick and Cassie headed up the long flight of stone steps that led to the top of Jade Mountain Resort, it became apparent that her feet were way too tired and ankles way too wobbly from the buttery nipples to keep her high heels on. The stone was cool and felt heavenly on the soles of her feet. Her thighs burned from climbing the steps so many times over the past three days, but every time, the expedition had been worth it. The location was undeniably the most spectacular setting ever. Liz was right. This romantic venue should be the perfect place to get pregnant, or at least get plenty of practice trying.

Entering the open-aired room, Cassie was greeted with the smell of incense that housekeeping lit nightly to ward off mosquitos. While draped mosquito netting on a four-poster bed was historically a romantic statement, Cassie had quickly learned its true purpose the past few days. Thankfully, high on the mountain top, the bugs weren't as bad as downhill. The room and view itself outweighed a few mosquitos, though. The private pool was glowing a vibrant blue hue, and with the help of the bright full moon, she could still make out the outline of the distant Piton mountains. As she released the side zipper of her dress, she let it peel off her sticky tan skin and fall to the floor. Sliding immediately into the damp sheets from the insurmountable humidity, she caught Rick standing on the opposite side of the bed smiling at her and staring at her naked body. "No pj's tonight, eh?" he quizzed as he followed suit.

"Are you complaining, Mr. Buchanon?" Cassie sexily taunted her husband. "Why bother when there's no air conditioning and its eighty degrees? Besides, it would just be that much more work taking them off in the morning." She winked at him as she rolled over to turn out the lights.

CHAPTER THREE

Cassie

DAMP, COOL AIR blew into the room off the Pitons, pushing the white mosquito netting onto Cassie's naked body, waking her from a peaceful slumber. The scent of the ever-blooming flowers surrounding the mountainside billowed in as well, indicating that the incense was long gone and thankfully, so were the bugs. Cassie's hand skimmed across the cool sheets to find Rick, his back to her, still sleeping quietly. She moved in closer to him, glancing at the few gray hairs that were starting to appear around his temples, perfectly illuminated in stark contrast to the surrounding dark brown. His skin was soft and damp and smelled of his natural scent mixed with leftover cologne from the previous night. Every muscle in his back was completely outlined like a black and white sketch from an anatomy textbook. Cassie smiled as she caught a glimpse of the top of his buttocks peeking out from under the single white sheet that draped haphazardly across his sun-kissed body. Her curious hand snuck under the sheet around him as the palm of her hand was greeted by his morning peak.

"I'm surprised you woke up before me, Dr. Buchanon. You must be anxious for something," Rick chuckled as he rolled over to face his wife.

"Maybe. How could you tell?" She smiled at his flirtatious and slightly arrogant remark. It was justified. Adonis had every right to be conceited. Cassie giggled while his morning stubble tickled her lips and neck as they assumed their all too familiar positioning. It wasn't long before Cassie felt his warmth inside her, triggering her to follow along in climax.

"Good thing you're quick on your feet this morning, because all of this scheduling and restriction doesn't give me much for stamina," Rick justified his brief performance with Cassie's micromanagement of their sex life as he planted a kiss on her forehead. Her heart sank at the thought of how much their intimacy had changed. She knew he didn't mean anything malicious by his comment, but he was right. She had planned their time in the sheets to the proficiency level of a Martha Stewart day calendar. Thankfully, his playful charm shifted her thoughts as her attention was drawn to the handsome naked man jumping to his feet and scurrying off to the wet bar.

"You stay here." He soon presented her a cup of water with the look, skill, and precision of a cabana boy. "I'm sure you need to rehydrate after all of those drinks last night, you party animal," Rick teased.

Cassie raised onto her elbows and reached for the cup, thankful for the bottled waters they had bought yesterday at the market.

"Why don't you get a little bit more sleep? It's still early and I promised Liz yesterday that I would meet her at the gym this morning to help her train," Rick proposed.

"I may take you up on that one," she agreed without debate, falling back onto the cool sheets, noticing the appearance of a dull headache and faint caramel taste in her mouth that made her throat tingle with nausea. "I'll meet you guys down at the beach in an hour or so if that's okay."

"Take your time, Dr. Buchanon. We have all day to enjoy the resort, and don't forget that John, Hal, and I are going sea kayaking in the cove around lunchtime."

———◆———

tink tink tink.

Cassie jumped up from a dead sleep, startled by the chimes of her phone alarm clock. *Oh, crap. What time is it?* They hadn't had cell service since they'd arrived in St. Lucia, nor had they had the need to set an alarm clock. It was a vacation, after all. Typically, the alarm on her phone fell on deaf ears, but without having heard it in days, it was foreign enough again to quickly catch her attention.

The screen on her phone showed a fertility calendar reminder notification:

12pm: Bang Your Husband.

"Efficiently completed, thank you very much," Cassie stated proudly. Despite the phone's uselessness in communication with the real world, she was thankful for the alarm. Otherwise, she would have slept well into the afternoon. She pushed the mosquito netting to the side, her still-sore feet touching the polished dark wood floors. Walking over to the infinity pool, Cassie made the impromptu decision to jump in.

The cool water engulfed her naked body, sending an intense wakeup call to her lymphatic system that was desperately trying to cure the last remnants of her lingering hangover. Cassie opened her eyes underwater to mystical blue and green glass tiles, the sun reflecting off them like sea glass. Her soul ached to bottle up this serenity and tuck it away for the real world, one overridden with work and stress. She felt the human strain for breath in her chest forcing her to rise for air.

"Just breathe, Cassie," she commanded herself. "It's all going to fall into place one day." Spiraling thoughts of babies and marriage and life and what the purpose was of all her recent roadblocks swirled in her brain. She had coasted through life fairly smoothly until now, so she yearned to find answers to the upheaval. Swimming to the infinity edge, she rested her arms and chin on the picturesque ledge, focusing her gaze on the pink bougainvillea that grew like weeds there. Sarah had used them to her advantage for the beautiful beachfront ceremony. The multitude of pink blooms had draped magnificently over the pergola, framing the breathtaking turquoise of the oceanic backdrop. As much as Cassie wanted to stay and try to solve all of her life problems in one fell swoop, Sarah and Liz would be wondering where she was. Security would surely be arriving any minute to check on her.

Hopefully, Rick told them I was going to get some rest. I can only imagine they're feeling just as hungover as me, especially Liz. After all, her half-pint body frame took way more shots than any of us. She wondered how Liz had held up with her triathlon training this morning. She prayed Rick had had a little sympathy for her condition.

Making her way into the teak-and-stone-clad bathroom, Cassie was starting to see the appeal to nudists on the whole naked thing. It was pretty convenient. As she turned to plunge her blonde curls under the streaming shower, she caught a glimpse of her backside in the mirror. *Damn. What did I run into last night? Surely that isn't from the jettie escapade?* As she ran her hand across the bluish-green mark, the familiar torso twist jarred her memory. The culprit: the fertility shot she had administered to herself the previous morning. Cassie shuddered at the thought of the massive needle. Despite having given what seemed like a million injections over the years as a physician, there was still something unsettling about stabbing yourself with a two-inch needle. *Hopefully, my pain and markings won't go in vain this time. What did the doctor say? I need to wait fourteen days before a pregnancy blood test can be taken if I don't start my period before then?*

Long gone were the days of the good old pee-on-a-stick pregnancy test. Cassie hated to think of all the money she had spent on the whole process. She could have funded a trip to the French Riviera with what she had spent over the past two years on ovulation predictors and pregnancy tests. After all, EPT claimed to be the "earliest indicator, with detection up to five days before your missed period." This cruelly marketed to the impatient, hopeful women, praying to see two blue lines. So, like clockwork, Cassie, like other mommy-hopefuls, had tested every day for five days, time and time again, only to be disappointed by the blood on her cute little thongs.

It was a good ten-minute walk from their suite to the beach at the base of the mountain. Cassie tucked her beach hat into her tote, realizing that her headache had finally simmered. She didn't want to risk any extra pressure on her skull possibly reawakening the monster. She donned her large-framed tortoise sunglasses and gave herself one last glance in the foyer mirror before heading to the beach. The trek down the stone steps was a familiar one, and thankfully came a little easier while sober. Cassie easily spotted Liz and Sarah stretched out on the bright royal blue resort beach chairs. Sarah's Danish heritage ensured that she wore a large-brimmed hat with all the sunscreen she could afford. She typically plopped herself under an umbrella, so she was easy to find. Liz, being olive skinned and brunette, was the total opposite—a sun goddess. Cassie and Sarah had their suspicions that she hid pure baby oil in sunscreen-marked packaging to keep them from nagging her about melanoma and wrinkles.

"Liz, you're a plastic surgeon, for God's sake. You know what the sun does to your skin. You spend your day correcting people's bad habits. How do you sleep at night with such sun-drenched skin? More importantly, how do you look your patients in the eyes when you push your over-priced sunscreen on them?" Sarah had questioned on more than one occasion. Liz never seemed fazed over the judgment from her friends.

"Oh, Sarah, you gotta live a little. Besides, I wasn't meant to be pale. I'm not me without a tan," she would brush off easily, typically with a smile and a wink. Cassie had assumed it was because she knew she had John, her partner in their husband/wife duo plastics practice, at her disposal to correct her bad choices when she needed it. Not everyone had that luxury.

"Well, here is Sleeping Beauty herself," Liz yelled over the crashing waves. "You're totally missing the show. The guys are about to kill themselves out there." Cassie looked into the cove to see large kite-looking contraptions and ant-sized men desperately trying to hang on to them while poorly balancing on surf boards.

"Wind sailing? Rick has been trying forever to get me to let him do this, but I told him I didn't have time to take care of him when he breaks his back. And I need his pelvis to work at least until I get pregnant. Hope Hal already added you as his beneficiary, Sarah. What happened to sea kayaking?" Cassie squinted against the bright sun that was starting to reawaken her headache despite the valiant effort of the large-framed sunglasses that shielded her eyes, as she tucked quickly into the seat under an umbrella that Sarah had kindly saved for her.

"Oh, been there, done that already. They did that for about an hour and got bored. We still hadn't seen the likes of you, so I guess Rick decided there was safety in numbers, and you weren't around to veto it." Sarah giggled as she turned to see the only wind kite left standing strike into the water with limbs flying into the air.

"Another one bites the dust. You really are missing a great show, Cas. These guys are going to be so sore they won't walk for a week." Liz laughed, noticing Cassie's grimace from the sun. "You look like you could use a drink, sweetie. You know my mantra: 'hair of the dog.' Kai!" Liz yelled and waved her arms at the familiar handsome St. Lucian bartender from the night before.

"Oh, so you're on a first name basis with the bartender now?"

"Yes, Cas. We waited so long for your ass to get down here, we decided to get started on our recovery process without you. Besides, I felt like it was only proper to be on a first name basis with such a brilliant mixologist." Liz winked at Kai and his bulging biceps, looking as focused as a tiger on her prey. "Seriously, ladies, have you ever had such a delicious shot in all of our taste-testing years? It's no wonder we all feel like ass today. Those buttery nipples went down like milkshakes."

"Yeah, now those milkshakes are wreaking havoc on my skull. The aftermath is not so delicious." Kai appeared beside Cassie to take her order. "I'll have a blueberry vodka with a splash of soda, please."

"*PaPow!* That's my girl. You're going hard early." Liz fist pumped the bright blue sky with Mike Tyson skills.

"I need something strong to push me past this one, ladies. Besides, this could be one of my last weekends to party for a while," Cassie said, shrugging her shoulders before grabbing Sarah's mimosa and taking a generous sip, hoping her morning efforts with Rick would lead to Babyville this time.

"Attagirl! Make that two, please, Kai." The brilliant mixologist nodded to Liz and smiled flirtatiously at Cassie and Sarah before heading back to his cabana bar.

"Liz, seriously? He's a kid. You wouldn't know what to do with him," Sarah said, rolling her eyes.

"Oh, I'm sure I could figure it out." Liz pulled her sunglasses down onto her nose to get one last look at Kai as he walked away.

Cassie could see in the daylight and with sober eyes that he was much younger than she had remembered from the previous night. He couldn't have been much older than twenty-one. "Oh, to be young again. Who knew all of those years ago when I was being promiscuous and trying to *not* get pregnant that I was actually wasting all of my good eggs? If I had known then what I know now, I would have frozen those suckers," Cassie huffed. "Every time I see my fertility doctor, he asks me my age. As if he doesn't have it in my chart, right under his nose, and didn't just ask me that very question at my *previous* ultrasound appointment two days prior. I think he wants me to say it out loud just so I can't deny myself full knowledge of my *premature ovarian failure*, as he likes repeating. I will never forget, at our consult with him, he looked me straight in the eyes and said, 'You know, these things have been working since you were thirteen.' Well, sue me for trying to do things the *right way*—you know, get my doctorate, start my career, find my husband. I guess if I had gotten knocked up earlier in life, I would have different troubles." Cassie shrugged her shoulders. "But enough about that. Let's talk about more important things." She turned to the new bride. "Sarah, you looked gorgeous last night, and the ceremony was absolutely perfect. I'm so happy for you. You waited for Mr. Right and it paid off, my dear."

Cassie reached over and grabbed Sarah's hand, eyeing her gorgeous new diamond wedding band. It suited her perfectly. A simple gold band with round diamonds embedded in it. Cassie smiled, remembering when her wedding rings looked like that, polished and shiny, not yet tarnished by time and copious amounts of hand sanitizer due to her career as a doctor.

"Thank you. It was everything I had ever imagined. Hal is wonderful and having you two here means everything to me."

"We wouldn't have missed it for the world, Sarah." Cassie was taken aback by Sarah's apologetic tone.

"I know, I just realize how tough it is with you and Rick right now, trying to get pregnant. Liz told me that you've had to miss a lot of work and reschedule patients to see the fertility doctor every few days. I'm sure it probably wasn't convenient for you to be here right now."

"Sarah, nothing is more important than you at this very moment," Cassie reassured her friend. As if on cue, Kai returned with their order.

"Cheers to Mrs. Hal Lutz and Cassie laying an egg." Liz raised her drink and the three of them toasted her blunt remark. "I guess John and I have taken so much for granted in our marriage. As much as we fucked the first two years we were together, it's a wonder we aren't the damn Duggars. I can remember skipping class sometimes just to go back to our apartment and get a quickie in. Ah, those were the days." Liz gazed onto the waves to see her husband trying unsuccessfully to balance on the surfboard.

"Yeah, you and John were almost as bad as Cassie and Dylan. Remember ladies, we all lived together. It's a wonder I ever got sleep between the banging noises coming from your two bedrooms," Sarah laughed.

"Cassie and Big Dick Dylan…." Liz trailed off in a sarcastic reminiscent tone. They all three laughed at their crude but accurate nickname for him. "Do you ever hear from him, Cas? Everyone thought you two were a sure thing. I heard he was practicing ENT in Atlanta."

"I haven't heard from him since we broke up after our ENT residency at Emory," she shrugged. "It's strange and depressing to think that someone you spent years dating, making love to, spending holidays with, planning your future with, suddenly can become nonexistent in your life. Dating sure is a screwed-up thing," Cassie said shaking her head. "I haven't laid eyes on him since we ended. We talked on the phone a few times, but it was just too painful to try and open up that door again."

"What happened? I never really knew," Sarah asked as she polished off the remnants Cassie had left her of her mimosa.

"Priorities. I never felt first. There was always some-thing more pressing—school, work, rotations, family, friends. I felt like a leftover. So, I pushed—probably too hard at times—which led to fights. We fought as pas-sionately as we loved. And trust me, that was ridiculously intense," Cassie smiled, thinking of her dreams of late that had been stirring up her memories of their fervent love affair. "Maybe the timing wasn't right? Who knows? I do think about him sometimes and wonder how he is, but I am one hundred percent certain that we made the right decision to part ways," Cassie stated matter-of-factly, try-ing to override her very own doubts. "The even stranger thing is that since I've been on fertility hormones, I've had dreams about him nonstop. It's crazy. Why would I dream about a guy from years ago?" Cassie finally felt the need to confess to her most trusted friends. Maybe if she told them, they could help reassure her that this was nor-mal and that she had indeed picked the right path in life.

"Well, are they juicy?" Liz pried, as Sarah rolled her eyes. "What? She was totally hooked on his big dick. I would probably dream about that thing too. We had a nickname for it. What was it?"

"Ana," Cassie replied begrudgingly.

"That's right! Anaconda. See, you can't forget a dick with a name."

"Let's halt on the ex-lover, big-dick talk for now, Liz," Cassie said, disappointed in the lack of clarity she had hoped her friends would provide. She tipped her nearly empty glass toward the christened jetties from the night before to their husband trio. She could see the guys had finally given up on windsurfing as they walked up the beach with their surfboards and kites in tow, looking like drowned puppies with their tails between their legs.

"Ouch. They're going to need some drinks, too. Kai!"

Cassie was thankful for her floppy beach hat as the blinding sun snuck through the tiny holes between the woven straw. The waves rocked her gently as she laid sunbathing on the bow of the boat. The seagulls squawked above her in the sky, probably following the fish, just like Dylan. The sound of his cast rung familiarly in her ears as another baited hook plunged into the deep blue ocean. Grouper. That was what was on the menu for the evening, given they got lucky and caught one. If not, Cassie was certain in her abilities to coax him into dinner at a nice restaurant.

"Heck, yes!" She heard Dylan's excitement as he set the hook in some poor creature. She tipped the straw hat up to see him fighting something that appeared to be buried at the bottom of the sea. Cassie couldn't take her eyes off of him. He looked so sexy with his biceps and shoulders bulging to reel in the catch. He was something to behold with his jet back hair and tall, fit stature. He turned to smile at her with his gleaming white smile highlighted by the tan he had acquired from all the hours spent on his new boat. There was something so captivating about seeing a man in his primitive hunter-gatherer mode. Cassie discreetly gazed around to see if anyone had decided to crash their fishing hole. No boat, land, or airplane for as far as the eye could see. Just crystal blue water surrounding their little love boat. Reaching behind her neck and loosening the tie, Cassie tossed her already barely-existing triangle bikini top to the floor of the boat and quietly laid back down, covering her face with her hat, trying not to make a stir. It couldn't have been more than about a minute before a dark shadow blocked the sun sneaking through her straw hat.

"What kind of fish did you catch?" She smiled a guilty

grin as she tipped the brim of her hat up to face an overly-eager, handsome man practically panting on top of her.

"Not sure. I cut the line. Something over here caught my eye," Dylan stated matter-of-factly as he placed small kisses on her bare chest. She could feel his extra-large package brush against her inner thigh.

"Cassie, you are intoxicating," Dylan whispered as his nose stroked her neck. Chill bumps rose over her entire body and every hair was at attention. Her heartbeat was almost audible, and torture mounted as she waited desperately for him to enter her. The swaying and rocking of the boat increased, making it even more challenging to keep him close enough as she held him tighter, not wanting to let go.

Suddenly a huge splash of water came from nowhere…

———◆———

"Cassie! Cassie! Wake up!"

Cassie jumped up, her heart racing, to see her hat floating in the swimming pool next to her. Rick was rocking her float and Liz, John, Hal, and Sarah were all laughing hysterically at her startled reaction.

"You must have been having some hell of a dream. You were breathing so hard I could hear you on the other side of the pool. Are you okay?" Rick teased.

"Um, of course. I don't remember what I was dreaming about, but I guess it was pretty good," she lied, praying her red skin from the sun hid her blushed face. *Holy shit. Not again. This is the third dream about Dylan in the past few days.* Truthfully, she was secretly enjoying them. She peered over at Sarah and Liz to find them both winking and giggling. They were on to her ex-boyfriend fantasy. They must have figured out what she was breathing so heavy about from her true confessions earlier that day at the beach. Cassie shook her head no to them, signaling for them to knock it off.

"We need to get showered and dressed. We have dinner reservations at the rooftop of Jade Mountain in an hour," Rick reminded his wife of their farewell dinner for Sarah and Hal. The newlyweds were leaving for their honeymoon the following morning, while the Buchanons and Hamiltons headed back to Tampa to the real world.

As Cassie climbed out of the pool, she could hear Liz snicker. "Yeah, I think a cold shower would do you good, Cas," Liz mocked as she and Sarah both chuckled under their breath. If it hadn't been for her sunglasses, Cassie was sure her glare could have struck them both dead in that instant.

"I couldn't agree more, ladies," Hal reinforced innocently. Poor guy, he had no clue about the underlying source of humor as he wiped the sweat dripping from his nose. Sarah smiled at his innocent comment. "I must admit that I'm having air conditioning withdrawals. I have never considered myself one to be a prima donna, but this open-air situation is getting old."

"Oh, Hal, it gives you two lovebirds even more of an excuse to sleep naked," Liz coached as she and John gathered up their belongings. "Besides, you may as well enjoy the heat now because the bedroom only gets colder from now on." John's eyebrows furrowed at his wife's snide remark. Liz had always been somewhat demanding and high-maintenance, but Cassie was taken aback at her friend's jab. She had never noticed a lack of romance or attraction between John and Liz. They, of course, no longer had the youthful, uninhibited sexual aura that exuded from them when they were in their twenties, but they definitely had a more loving, flirtatious relationship than the majority of the married couples she knew.

Cassie's mind raced with concern and questions about Liz's comment as Rick prodded her with a slap on the rear. "Let's go, Dreamweaver." But he only broke her train of thought for a moment. *Liz is probably just being overdramatic. She's just pouting over a scuffle with John or something.* Cassie vowed to herself to probe further at dinner, though. Something wasn't settling right in her gut.

CHAPTER FOUR

Liz

LIZ'S MIND FELT numb. She wasn't sure if it was from the blueberry vodkas or the whirlwind of thoughts that had turned her brain into mush. As she mindlessly rummaged through her suitcase for dinner attire, searching through the last few unworn pieces, she felt John's hand slide around her waist from behind. Instantly, her body stiffened.

"Liz, what's wrong with you?" Liz turned to him, forcing a fake smile, trying to overshadow her cold response to his gesture.

"Oh, nothing. You just startled me, that's all," Liz explained quickly. She was surprised, too, at how visceral her reaction had become to his touch as her heart sank with guilt.

"I want to talk about your comment to Hal a few minutes ago. You know, about the bedroom only getting colder. What's going on with you? More importantly, what is going on with *us*?" John pried with desperation as he cupped her tan face gently in his hands.

Liz's heart pounded from fear that her guilt would surely give her away. Peeling slowly away from his grasp, she moved toward the shower, buying herself some time as she searched for the right words to say. "I was just kidding. I'm fine. We're fine." She pushed the untruthful words forcefully out of her mouth.

"I've known you for years. I can read you like a book.

Something is definitely off with you. Every time I try to touch you, you practically shudder. You're too stressed or too tired or too busy to have sex or spend any quality time with me, for that matter. Have I done something wrong? Do I need to do something different? Help me out here, babe," John begged his wife, standing at the bathroom door as she undressed for the shower.

"Life is just hard right now. The boys have been running me ragged with sports and school. The office always has one of us tied up with surgeries and weekend on-call shifts. And I'm nervous about this triathlon. It's not you, I promise." At least that part she could say with confidence, looking him in the eyes. The problem was her. John had been a blue-ribbon husband. But her heart yearned for something more. Something raw, passionate.

"I agree. Life is busy. So… on that note, I have a little surprise that might help us out." John smiled sneakily. "Don't be angry. I took a step outside of our business partner boundaries," he revealed slowly. "I figured it would be better to beg for forgiveness than ask for permission."

Liz turned to him before stepping into the shower, crossing her arms over her bare breasts, casting a suspicious glare. "What have you done?"

"Don't say no. Just think about it before you react, okay?"

"Okay. Just tell me," Liz said nervously, starting to get slightly annoyed at the suspense.

"I enlisted a headhunter to find us an associate surgeon…" John squeaked out quickly, and then held his breath as he waited for Liz's reaction. "Babe, it's what we need. It will give us more time together and give you more free time," he explained with a smile.

"I don't know. It sounds nice in theory, but how do we find someone that will fit in with us? Who's going to want to work for a husband and wife duo? And can we even afford it? Hiring an associate is no cheap feat," Liz questioned.

"That's up to the headhunter to find a fit for us. I ran the numbers, and we can definitely afford someone. So, just to let you know, we have someone coming next week to interview. Surprise!" John chuckled as Liz rolled her eyes.

"When exactly were you going to tell me this?" Liz's hands shifted to her hips as she stood aggravated and naked glaring at her husband.

"I didn't want you stressing about it during our trip here, so I was going to tell you on our way back, but right now seemed good. It's going to be great. Trust me." Liz's heart stopped as he muttered those words. *Trust me.* Forcing a smile and a nod, she turned to seek refuge in the shower. The words rang over and over in her ears as her mind flashed back to earlier that morning...

"Liz, you can do this. Just two more miles," Rick pushed.

"I can't. I'm done. There's no way I'm going to be able to do two more miles. Not today. Not after last night," Liz cried as her gait came to a halt and she bent over in exhaustion. Rick stopped, too, turning to her. Grabbing her chin, he lifted her face to his, planting a sexy sweaty kiss on her breathless lips.

"Yes, you can. *Trust me,*" he whispered, looking firmly into her eyes. Sliding his hand up the front of her sweat drenched shirt and then down between her thighs, her heartbeat raced to a level near cardiac arrest. "I can't stop thinking about you," Rick admitted as he kissed her neck.

"Rick. We can't. Not here. Not right now," Liz said breathlessly, leaning into his touch despite her words.

"Why not?" he argued, still continuing on his mission.

"What if someone sees us? Besides, Cassie needs you

this morning. I may be a shitty friend for sleeping with her husband, but spoiling her baby agenda will send me to an even deeper ring of the fires of hell." Liz pushed away from him.

Rick stood there, hanging his head in defeat. As he looked up at Liz, she wanted nothing more than to undress him right there in the tropical forest.

"I took care of Cassie's agenda already. She has me so scheduled I feel like a walking sperm donor."

Liz could see the sadness in his eyes. It was the same sadness she saw in the mirror. She ran her fingers through his hair, slicking back the sweaty strands.

"What are we doing?" she asked remorsefully. "How did we get here?"

Rick shook his head. "Not sure. No clue."

———◆———

As the water poured through her hair, Liz struggled to find answers. She loved John. She would never hurt him in a million years, or their boys for that matter. *Of all the people to cheat on your husband with, you just had to pick your best friend's husband. Great choice, Liz.* She decided that there were no correct answers or excuses for her actions, and most devastating was that she realized she couldn't confide in either of the two people she had always gone to for support. She would have to somehow weave her way through this midlife crisis alone.

———◆———

The dinner venue was plucked straight from *Travel + Leisure.* The rooftop view proved that they were in a bubble of luxury, dropped smack dab in the middle of tropical paradise. The sun was setting over the Pitons and the Caribbean in the distance. The white tablecloths reflected the dying sunlight and danced with a much-welcomed breeze. The entire property was decorated with intricately carved wood and colorful, locally-crafted glass tiles that topped architectural columns and lined the private swimming pools.

The candles and torches cast a beautiful glimmer on their sun-drenched bodies. Sarah appeared exhausted as the adrenaline-filled bridal rush had finally begun to wear off. She still possessed the glow of wedded bliss, but her eyes were heavy as she leaned on Hal's shoulder. Wrapping his arm around her, he planted a kiss on his new wife's temple. Liz smiled endearingly as she watched the two of them. Her gaze fell across the table to Rick. He was so dashingly handsome and polished. Her heart sank as she watched Cassie lean in to kiss him. "I love you, baby," she read from Cassie's lips as they whispered to Rick. Her heart sank even deeper as she watched his lips mutter the same words back with a loving smile. John's hand slid under the table and onto Liz's thigh. Startled, she jumped, knocking over her wine glass and spilling it onto her dress.

"Damnit!" she yelled, pushing back from the table. As she grabbed for a napkin to clean her wine-drenched dress, she caught sight of John's bewildered face. Her heart sank knowing she'd done it again. Angry at herself for her now repeated reaction to John's touch, coupled with her jealousy from watching Cassie and Rick's display of affection, Liz stood to flee and find some sort of refuge from the awkwardness.

"Excuse me, please." She looked at John and her friends apologetically. Her outburst was uncalled for. Frustrated and embarrassed, she scurried off to the ladies' room to try and pull herself together physically and mentally.

Liz heard footsteps following her. The sound of high heels clicking on stone tiles indicated that it was her best friend coming for interrogation. "What, Cassie? I'm fine," she snapped over her shoulder.

"Liz, I just wanted to talk to you alone. Is everything

okay with you and John? I noticed today that you seemed agitated with him, and you've made several snarky comments about your marriage. Are you all okay?"

"Of course, we are." Liz stopped in her tracks, spinning around, forcing the corners of her mouth upward. As the breeze caught her dark brown hair, causing her to turn away from the gust of wind, Liz saw Cassie squint suspiciously, clearly not believing her answer.

Putting her arm around Liz's stiff body, Cassie whispered in her ear, "Lizzie, you can't fool your best friend. I'm always here for you."

Liz stared down at her wine-soaked dress, unable to make eye contact. Her heart ached at the fact that this was certainly one thing Cassie couldn't help her with. "Cas, someday when you and Rick have been with each other as long as John and I have, you'll come to a crossroads in your marriage. So far, for the majority of it, John and I have taken the same path and built an amazing life." She smiled softly, shifting her gaze sentimentally to her left hand and the diamond wedding bands that adorned it. "But the past few months have been different. I'm not sure what's happening, but it's like we're on two separate paths. Sure, we're cordial at work, and fully functional at home for the boys, but we're puppets performing our own lives on autopilot. I want some spice, some excitement. Something to make me feel sexy and young again. Not like an almost forty-year-old mom."

Cassie placed her fingers under her best friend's chin, tipping her head upward ensuring eye contact. "Well, first of all, you are a sexy, beautiful, successful plastic surgeon who just happens to make being an almost forty-year-old mom look glamourous. And by the way John looked at you last night on the dance floor, I don't think you have anything to worry about. You two looked pretty perfect to me."

Liz smiled at Cassie's attempt to make her feel better.

"Well, I suppose we are well-trained monkeys. We can sure put on a good show, especially with enough alcohol."

"Try to remember what attracted you to John all those years ago. Of course, your relationship is going to morph into different shapes over the years, but you still have an amazing marriage, and it takes work, sometimes more than other times. I haven't been married as long as you, but trust me, fertility treatment can sure put a damper on your sex life. I'm sure that sounds crazy, but it turns into a chore rather than a fun, spontaneous frolic in the sheets. Every relationship has challenges, and I'm sure that you will find a way to get back on the same path. This is just a slight detour."

Cassie's long arms embraced Liz as she planted a kiss on top of her head. Liz's mind whirled in response to Cassie's pep talk. *Slight detour? I guess you could call it that. I'm thinking more of a bumpy off-road expedition off the side of a cliff.*

CHAPTER FIVE

Cassie

*C*ASHEWS, WILD-CAUGHT SALMON, *garlic, aspara-gus, and sauvignon blanc. Check, check, check, check, and check.* Cassie quickly went over her mental grocery list while standing in line at the market. Liz and John were coming over for dinner, and Liz had been in full-blown triathlon mode. Rick had Liz on a strict diet during these final days before the competition. Cassie was all too familiar with the approved meals, having spent years preparing them for her super-competitive husband. The wine, of course, wasn't on the triathlon-approved diet list, but that wasn't something Liz was ever willing to give up.

Cassie hadn't seen Liz and John since they'd returned from St. Lucia, and she was beyond anxious to see how they were getting along. Cassie had called Liz earlier in the week and invited them over for dinner on Friday so she could assess the situation. And, selfishly, so that Liz could hook her up with Botox injections.

"Why don't you and John come over for dinner Friday night? And bring a bottle of Botox, please," Cassie snuck in quickly as she trailed off. Every month before her period was supposed to come was like the Last Supper: she drank her last bottle of wine for nine months, ate her last plate of sushi, and drank her last cup of caffeinated coffee. Botox injections were included in that category of pregnancy forbidden delicacies.

"Cassie, sometimes I think you only love me for the

free cosmetic services," Liz snickered.

"You figured me out," Cassie laughed. One of the many perks of having a plastic surgeon as your best friend was an unlimited amount of Botox, fillers, laser hair removal, microdermabrasion, and wonderful skin care products, all at cost. She hadn't gotten to the point of needing the big dogs yet, like face lifts and liposuction. She had been blessed with a nice 34C cup that had turned into a voluptuous D recently thanks to the multitude of hormones, so she had steered clear of the scalpel thus far, but she wasn't above it when the time came.

"That sounds great. We'll be there. Oh, but is it okay if we bring a guest? I forgot to tell you that John took it upon himself to decide that we needed an associate in our practice, and the headhunter he hired set the candidate to arrive Friday morning," Liz said, clearly annoyed. "John thinks I'm too stressed and that we need more time together, so this is his answer to all of our problems. I'm not so convinced just yet."

"Oh, that sounds like a great idea. I can't wait to meet him." Cassie was thankful to hear that John was on to Liz's weird behavior. Hopefully, they had done some talking and it would all work itself out soon.

"Her. It's a female doctor. Her name is Kelly, I think."

"Oh. Okay. Can't wait to meet *her*." Cassie sensed a bit of venom in Liz's words. She was certain that Liz could use the free time, but not so sure about her willingness to share her matriarchal position in her business. "Why don't the three of you come over after work? If I'm not home yet, then Rick should be there."

———◆———

As Cassie pulled up the short drive to her South Tampa home, she was surprised to find that Rick still hadn't returned from his trip yet. He had been out of town working in Houston and should have been home already.

Maybe his flight was delayed? I was hoping to have some alone time with him before John and Liz got here. But it wasn't looking like that was going to happen. She checked her phone to see if Rick had texted, but no luck.

She stumbled into the kitchen with arms full of groceries, hearing her cell phone beep inside her purse that was hanging on her shoulder. *It must be Rick,* she thought. She set the bags down on the large marble island in the center of the kitchen. As she tossed her purse onto the navy and white bistro barstool, she heard another beep coming from it. After retrieving her phone from the black hole that always seemed to engulf everything she needed to find, she saw a text from Rick, who had just landed at the airport and would be running a bit late. A second message came from Liz stating she was minutes away. Cassie wondered why she and John were driving separately when they were supposed to be coming straight from the office. *That's odd. Maybe one of them had to stay for an after-hours emergency. And don't they have the interview candidate with them today?* Cassie's mind wandered. She had no sooner gotten the groceries unpacked when she heard the back door shut and the bang of Liz's keys hitting the marble of the island. She didn't so much as say a word as she headed directly to the subzero to exchange a tiny bottle of Botox for a much larger bottle of wine.

"Hey," Cassie muttered sarcastically. "Bad day?"

"Nope," replied Liz without making eye contact, all while pouring a hefty glass of Sancerre. "Want some?" She tipped another empty wine glass to Cassie.

"Um, sure, but don't you want to make me gorgeous first before you get all drunk and shaky handed?" Cassie asked. The last thing she wanted was a crooked eyebrow for the next three months.

"Cas, I could do this with my eyes closed. Besides, I think I'm better with a drink or two. Calms my nerves."

"Kind of like how you get better at golf and bowling after a few drinks? I have seen that disaster firsthand, friend. I don't think so." Cassie grabbed the full wine glass out of Liz's hand and plopped down in the bistro bar chair, taking a hefty sip. Liz pursed her lips in annoyance but proceeded to administer what seemed like a hundred Botox beestings. Once she was done, Cassie headed to the bathroom to clean up before meal prepping and to empty out her bladder from the glass of wine she had snatched from Liz. *Where could Rick be? He must have gotten stuck in traffic.* She could hear Liz giggling in the other room. She was probably watching some stupid YouTube video she had found. Liz loved sending crude videos and memes on the reg. As much as Cassie made fun of her sick humor, she secretly did enjoy the laugh.

"What's so funny?" Cassie asked as she made her way to preheat the oven. "Another inappropriate meme?"

"Oh, nothing. Just checking my emails. Hey, have you heard from Sarah? Is it rude to FaceTime her while she is on her honeymoon?" Liz diverted.

"I don't think Sarah would mind. She probably expects us to. After all, we have to remind Hal where he stands in all of this. He married her, so that means he married us too," Cassie laughed.

"True. We can't let him think that just because she's his wife now that he gets her all to himself." Liz fist pumped the air and scurried off to the bathroom. Cassie couldn't help but laugh at Liz's swift shuffle, trying to make it there on time. Liz had been known to have a few accidents, especially after the boys. Somehow, her tiny frame had managed to carry and deliver both the ten-pound hulks naturally, but at a hefty price to her pelvic sling.

Cassie heard the bathroom door close just as the ping of a text sounded on Liz's phone. Grabbing it instinctively, thinking it must be John, Cassie's eyes nearly popped out of her head... *Oh, shit! That is definitely not John.* There, before her eyes, was a picture of a penis, a zoomed-in image of full-on manhood, and in primitive male-action mode to boot. Her head started to spin. She had only seen John naked once. It was a drunken night of strip poker combined with skinny dipping way back in med school days. The memory was fogged with time and alcohol, but unless John had been tanning naked and dying his pubic hair with Just For Men, this was not the towheaded John she knew and loved. Cassie quickly glanced to the top of the screen to see who it was from, knowing Liz would be coming back any second. No name, only the words *Favorite Mistake.*

Well, at least this penis has a clever name, she thought. Cassie heard Liz opening the bathroom door. About the same moment, Rick walked through the back door pulling behind him two suitcases full of work paraphernalia. She quickly tossed Liz's phone back onto the countertop, and guiltily shuffled it around, trying to recreate its exact previous placement. *Why am I embarrassed? Liz should be the one feeling guilty here. Not me,* Cassie coached herself as she tried to pull herself together. She must have worn a look of horror because Rick stopped dead in his tracks when he saw her. Just as he started to question the look plastered across her face, Liz entered the room and Cassie took the opportunity to quickly throw back a college-sized gulp from her wine glass.

"Something wrong, babe?" Rick asked as he kissed Cassie on the cheek.

"Who, me?" she scrambled nervously, trying to think of an excuse for her lack of poker face. "No, honey. I just wasn't expecting you for a few more minutes."

"I'm sorry. I figured you heard the door close behind me. Looks like you ladies have already hit the bottle," Rick said, disapprovingly. "Liz, you know I don't condone drinking while training." Liz smiled and gave him an eat shit look as she gulped down the last bit of Sancerre inhabiting her glass.

"We haven't had time to partake too much yet. Relax, okay? Liz just got here too. Liz, do you have an ETA for John?" Liz grabbed her phone to check for John's status. Cassie watched as Liz's eyes opened wide with shock seeing the large specimen of manly self-photography under her nose.

"What's wrong?" Cassie asked dumbly as she watched her friend quickly scramble to another screen.

"Oh, nothing really," Liz replied with a distracted tone. "He and Kelly just got tied up at the office. They'll be here shortly."

"Who's Kelly?" Rick asked.

"Oh, I forgot to tell you. Liz and John are adding an associate to their practice," Cassie said.

"Her name is Kelly Chandler," Liz mocked with an eye roll. "She is ridiculously smart and talented and pretty. I'm sure John is doing whatever he can to spend an extra ten minutes with her."

"I sense a little jealous bone. I'm sure you have nothing to worry about, Lizzie," Rick reassured as he squeezed Liz tightly in a bear hug, lifting her petite frame up off the ground.

"No, no jealousy. Just doubtful. I'm not convinced this will solve all of our life problems like John thinks it will," Liz said breathlessly as she squirmed to break free of Rick's clutch.

"A hot, smart, young female associate? Yeah, that's always a great idea." Rick chuckled sarcastically as he lowered Liz back to the ground. "Maybe you should limit the interviewees to old, hairy, overweight men," he added. Cassie could sense Liz's anxiety building. She silently agreed with Rick. This was destined to add even more fuel to the distressed marriage fire, but Cassie knew there was no way that John would ever have eyes for anyone but Liz. In all their years as friends, she had never seen him even so much as look at another woman, and the same went for Liz towards another man. But obviously today was a new era. Not only was her best friend insecure about another woman being around John, but she was also getting penis sexts from an incognito *Favorite Mistake*. Red flags swarmed in Cassie's mind like buzzards.

"Rick, stop it. Liz, John has only loved one woman in his life, and that is *you*, my dear," Cassie reassured her as she made her way to the cabinet, her mind spinning faster than the food processor she was seeking to find. Liz shrugged her shoulders doubtfully as Rick thankfully changed the subject, beckoning her to the pergola-covered terrace to discuss their final week's training schedule before the big race. Cassie was relieved. She was becoming paranoid that her thoughts were loud enough to escape her brain through her ears. *What the hell? A dick pic! A jealous Liz?* None of this made sense. She needed more wine to calm her nerves.

Filling her glass to the brim, she heard John and an unfamiliar female voice coming through the back door. Both were laughing as they made their way into the kitchen. Cassie pulled together a cordial hostess smile and greeted the tall, thin blonde with a welcoming hug.

"Cassie, this is Kelly. She's from upstate New York and is interviewing for a position in our practice," John proudly introduced.

She eyed the gorgeous guest while handing her a poured glass of wine, and she could see why Liz may have been a slight bit jealous. Kelly was nothing shy of Victoria's Secret model status. Her platinum hair was cut into a short, sexy bob, framing her stunning symmetrical face. Her small but chiseled features were perfect, her skin flawless. And while she was professionally dressed in slacks and a tailored collared shirt that popped open just enough to show off her voluptuous chest, there was no denying that the figure that resided underneath was fit for a centerfold.

"It's so nice to meet you, Kelly. I can't wait to hear all about your day. I'm sure you're exhausted." Cassie motioned to the terrace where Rick and Liz were seated. Cassie saw through the glass of the French doors that Liz had acknowledged their arrival as her face turned from a smile to a look of defeat.

"I could easily get used to this weather," Kelly remarked as they stepped outside. "Upstate New York only has a few months of weather like this. I'm ready to put winter coats and snow shovels in my past."

They all agreed it was an unbelievably gorgeous Tampa evening. She and Rick loved sitting outdoors at night and having a glass of wine after a long day at work. They were one of the lucky few that possessed a backyard in South Tampa. Theirs was adorned with large shrubs and tall bamboo that created a private sanctuary. The pergola was draped with romantic white string lights and fitted with paddle fans for relief from the harsh Florida heat. Even the evenings could get toasty, but this one was perfect with a welcoming breeze.

The menu was a hit, and, despite the intrusion of an incredibly attractive fifth wheel, it turned out to be a fun evening. A few cocktails seemed to take the edge off everyone, as the conversation got easier to maneuver. They all started to feel the weight of the week as yawns crept into the conversation. Liz and Cassie cleared the outdoor table and headed to the kitchen for their regular dishwashing chores. Cassie washed and Liz did the drying.

"She seems lovely," Cassie said gently as she handed Liz the first clean dish.

"Yeah, she's pretty perfect," Liz cheered sarcastically.

"Come on. What's with you these days? Do you really think John would ever cheat? He adores you. I haven't ever seen you like this."

"No, Cassie. He's absolutely fucking perfect. And I'm just a huge piece of shit. I'm the wife that's insecure and yearns to feel passion and heat that doesn't come from a twenty-year relationship. That's what's wrong. There. You happy?" Liz snapped, tossing the dish towel onto the counter. Cassie could see the tears welling up in Liz's eyes. Her heart ached at Liz's rawness. *Maybe that's the problem? Maybe she feels unattractive? It makes sense. She is over-exercising, undereating, and overanalyzing.* Just then a ring came from the sofa table. Liz's eyes darted to her phone. Cassie's heart skipped a beat. *Was it Liz's Favorite Mistake?*

Liz smiled as she swiped to answer. An all too familiar voice came from the phone.

"Hey, Mrs. Lutz," Liz screeched. "Did you pull yourself away from that hunk of love long enough to check in with your besties?" Liz turned the screen toward Cassie and her wet dish hands.

Cassie breathed a sigh of relief for the change of subject. *Thank God. Sarah makes things better. That's exactly who I need to talk to about all of this.* Sarah was wise beyond her years and always seemed to have the right answers. Cassie decided to wait until after Sarah got back to Savannah. The last thing she wanted to do was cause any negative distraction during her friend's honeymoon. Being the most level-headed of the trio, she was certain Sarah could fix it all.

"Oh, I miss my girls," Sarah exclaimed. Liz and Cassie could see Hal in the background, waving and smiling. "And my boys," she added as John and Rick made their way into the living room and onto Liz's screen.

"Why are you calling us? You need to tend to your husband," John ordered Sarah as Liz rolled her eyes at his patriarchal comment.

"Don't you worry, Johnny boy. Hal is perfectly satisfied." Sarah giggled while Hal blushed boyishly.

"That's my girl," John winked, giving her an approving thumbs up.

After a short synopsis of the honeymoon, they bid Sarah farewell, blew them goodbye kisses, and vowed to visit within the month. Rick and Cassie showed their guests to the door and made their way to their own honeymoon suite.

"Baby, have you noticed something weird with John and Liz?" Cassie mumbled between toothpaste bubbles as she stood over the sink.

"No, why?" Rick stood behind Cassie, kissing her neck, seemingly unfazed by her question. While she was aroused by his efforts, she was also distracted with thoughts of Liz's promiscuity. His hand crept into the front of her black lace panties, and she found it increasingly difficult to keep her train of thought and proper toothbrushing technique.

"Oh, no reason," she muttered breathlessly, completely distracted at this point by his touch. Her concern for Liz quickly drifted away as she spun around to see the handsome face of her husband that she had missed for the past few days.

"I missed you," Rick whispered.

"Me too. I was so upset that you were late getting home tonight. I wanted some time with you before everyone got here," she said as he scooped her up in his arms, carrying her over to their bed.

"That's the thing about those darn airplanes. You can't drive them yourself," Rick said, tossing her onto the bed like a sack of potatoes.

"Easy there, mister. I could be with child," Cassie scolded. Realizing her tone by the look on Rick's face, she shot him a smile, playing off her comment. But she knew it bothered him. "I'm sorry, baby. I didn't mean to snap at you. Come here," she motioned Rick to lay beside her on the bed.

"Cas, can't we have just one day without talking about having a baby? Can't we make love like we used to?" Rick plopped onto the bed beside her, resting his head on his arm. Cassie knew what he meant. Their sex life had taken a big hit in the last few years.

"Yep. Let's start right now." She smiled at him. "Now come over here and fuck the hell out of me."

Rick's eyes got big at her bold direction.

"Yes, ma'am," he grunted, crawling on top of his wife. It wasn't long before they were tangled up in their bed. For the first time in as long as she could remember, they weren't on an agenda. They were there, in the present, not in hopes of the future and what it might bring.

Later, as Cassie lay staring at her husband as he slept peacefully, her thoughts raced back to her conversation that night with Liz. She had seemed so raw, so broken. She prayed she and Rick weren't in route to the same place in their marriage. Maybe that's all it was, just a new phase of their marriage. But there was the wildcard: the Favorite Mistake. Cassie hoped it was just innocent flirting and that Liz hadn't crossed a line she would regret. However, there was no denying the magnitude of the image, *literally*.

CHAPTER SIX

Cassie

CASSIE HAD NEVER been a fan of hospital cafeteria food. Not in med school, not in residency, and definitely not now. But after making it through her first two surgeries with her stomach howling and another patient being prepped, it was better than nothing, so she headed to the cafeteria for a quick snack. Her monstrous appetite was eyeing the chocolate bars, but her relentless quest to maintain her slim figure overrode the desire. As she paid for the overpriced banana and yogurt, she spotted John and Kelly sitting at a table with the hospital's surgical director, Dr. Bradley. Kelly and her long, super-toned arm waved Cassie over.

"Kelly, please don't make your decision on this job based on the cafeteria food," Cassie pleaded as John nodded in agreement while the smell of greasy chicken nuggets filled the air.

"But the coffee is damn good," John professed, holding high his Styrofoam cup. "At least they have their priorities straight. We were just about to take Kelly on a tour of the hospital, Cas. Would you like to join us? I know this is your surgery day. You could show Kelly the OR."

"That sounds great. But is there a way I can steal you for a minute, John? I need to run something by you."

"Of course," John agreed, asking Dr. Bradley to start the tour with Kelly. "We'll catch you guys on the second floor if that's okay, Kelly?" Kelly obliged John's request.

Cassie waited until the two were out of earshot before she slid onto the chair across from John, leaning in toward him, motioning him to come closer, insinuating a sensitive topic.

"What's up, chick?" John teased. "Need a face lift or something?"

"Not yet." Cassie narrowed her eyes at John's poke. "Have you noticed anything different with Liz? I'm worried about her. She seems weird."

John's eyes drifted down to his coffee cup and Cassie watched his Adam's apple move up his neck with force as he took a deep swallow. "Cas, you've known Liz and I since day one of our relationship. It's always been super easy. We live together, work together, practically shit together. We're pretty much one cohesive being. Sure, we've had our fights and our struggles, but this is different. I feel like she's going through something I can't pinpoint. Believe me, I've tried to figure it out. She isn't budging. She clams up and goes off by herself. She's even closed herself off from the boys at times. I told them Mom is stressed from work, which I thought was the problem. That's why I suggested an associate. I thought maybe she didn't have enough time for herself. I keep hoping once she can cut back at work, she'll be recharged and get back to her old self again. Has she said anything to you?"

Cassie tried to hide her internal discomfort as the thought of the dick pic swirled in her mind guiltily. She hated lying to her friend. He seemed so desperate to salvage his marriage. It was so characteristic of him to be superman and swoop in to rescue his wife.

"No, not really," she lied. "But she doesn't seem herself and I thought maybe there was something going on." Cassie grabbed his hands that were cradling the coffee cup and promised to get to the bottom of it. John gave her a thankful nod as she stood to return to the OR and meet up with Kelly and Dr. Bradley. Her heart sunk as she turned and walked away. She knew she may have just made a promise she couldn't keep.

———————◆———————

Cassie's phone chirped at least four times in a row in her pocket as she stood outside the OR. She excused herself from Kelly, fully expecting it to be the nurses' station. There were three patients in recovery, and it was about time for them to be dismissed. Surprisingly, it wasn't them. Her phone showed three messages from Liz and one from Rick. Typical. Liz was the most intense texter ever. She was notorious for sending multiple texts, all individual thoughts, all ending with exclamation points. Cassie hadn't determined if she was just impatient and prematurely hit the send button before completing all of her thoughts, or if she wanted multiple pings to go off, hoping to get Cassie's attention sooner.

Rick's message was the usual Monday night text. *Sushi or Pizza?* Cassie debated. Both sounded amazing, as the yogurt and banana were already losing their fill.

Pizza for the win, she replied, then scrolled on to see what was so pressing with Liz that she felt the need to send three texts in a row.

Hey!

I heard you ran into John and Kelly in the caf?

Did they look suspicious, like they were into each other?

Heat steamed from Cassie's face. It took every ounce of willpower she had to keep from texting back more truth than Liz wanted to see. *Wtf. What kind of nerve does she have to ask me that? She has Mr. Favorite Mistake texting her his erection pictures and she's worried about what her husband was doing at the lunch table?* Cassie's mind whirled with rage. She would love to put Liz in her place—especially after talking to John and knowing how distraught he was—but Liz would just shut her out, and that was the last thing Cassie wanted to happen. She needed Liz's trust to get to the bottom of what she was going through if there was any hope of salvaging her friends' marriage.

Yep. Saw them. Gave Kelly a tour of the OR. Are you for real? No, they weren't holding hands at the lunch table. She was very professional and seemed excited that you and John had offered her the position. I think she will accept your offer. She loves it here. And I really like her. You should too.

Uncharacteristically, Liz answered back with a single text: an eye roll emoji. Cassie couldn't help but think that maybe Liz's own actions were causing her paranoia. After all, that would be a way for Liz to make herself feel less guilty. She decided that pizza, yoga pants, and her couch would make her Monday much better, and to leave dissecting Liz's comments well enough alone for now.

———◆———

"Oh…my…gosh. This pizza might make up for the shitty day I had, babe," Cassie mumbled through the wad of cheese and crust she had stuffed into her mouth. Rick handed her a glass of sauvignon blanc and plopped down on the couch beside her. Remote in hand, he flipped predictably to ESPN to check scores and updates.

"Shouldn't I be the one carbing up for this weekend?" he chuckled as he wiped a big clump of pizza sauce from her chin. Rick must have thought she sounded like a scavenger as he stopped and stared at her overstuffed mouth with amazement.

"Shitty day. Pizza make wifey feel better," Cassie stated in her best cavewoman voice. "I saw Kelly today touring the hospital with John. I think she's taking the job. I really like her. She seems like she would fit in with all of us." Cassie paused before she let the next sentence roll off her tongue. She didn't want to disclose any information. She didn't need her husband accidentally leaking any information to Liz at a training session. But she wanted to see what Rick would think about Liz's accusations.

"So, Liz seems a little jealous of Kelly. She texted me like a crazy woman today to see if I thought she and John were into each other," Cassie nonchalantly mentioned as she took another cavewoman-sized bite. She watched as Rick huffed under his breath. "And remember the other night when we had them over for dinner how odd she seemed? Is it just me or is she acting extra high-maintenance lately?"

"No more than the typical, over-the-top Liz that we know and love," he said sarcastically.

"Has she been weird with you when she's training?" Cassie pried.

"Nothing in particular. Just super competitive. Okay, here is an example. So, you know how triathlons require the competitors to write their race numbers on their arms and legs in permanent marker and their age on the backs of their legs?" Cassie nodded, encouraging him to go on. "She actually told me she thought about dropping out of the race because of that. I thought she was going to have a panic attack. She said she was absolutely, positively not writing her age on her leg for everyone to see. You and I both know she looks amazing for her age, as she should, being that she's a plastic surgeon and married to one. I told her she had nothing to be ashamed of and that most women her age would kill to look like her. I finally calmed her down, but I bet she puts a fake age on her leg on race day." Rick stuck his hand out, wagering a bet sealed with a shake.

Cassie stared at him, baffled, taking his hand to accept the bet. "Really? She said that? I've never seen her so paranoid and insecure. For goodness sakes, there will be women twice her age competing against her."

"Sometimes people turn into versions of themselves that you never expected," Rick said softly. A twinge of guilt raced through Cassie's heart. He was right. She had turned into a momzilla version of herself that she wasn't too proud of. Her insecurities had even led her to question her marriage.

"Yeah. I guess you're right." Cassie snuggled in close to Rick, feeling ashamed for becoming something she had never expected to be—a wife with an agenda that extended far beyond the simple pleasures of love.

CHAPTER SEVEN

Cassie

"NO, NO," JOHN assured his wife. "You two go ahead. Cassie and I will save a place for you and Rick at the bar." Giving them the thumbs up, Cassie shooed Rick and Liz away. Race weekend was finally here, and John and Cassie were thankful to be part of the cheering squad and not tangled up in the intense hoopla of the event. Liz had been adamant that they get to Charleston a whole day early to scout out the race-course.

Cassie had become increasingly annoyed with Liz's overachiever antics as the week progressed. They'd been fueled by even more paranoia over Kelly accepting the job. "It's a sprint triathlon, not an Ironman, for God's sake," Cassie had muttered to Rick as he relayed Liz's training demands. Liz had insisted that she and Rick do a short swim in the lake and a trial bike ride on the actual race trail. Cassie and John had decided to walk the Battery and admire the historical homes while their counterparts were off training. Cassie had kept the conversation light up until they finally ended their excursion seated at the Cypress Restaurant's bar. The alone time with John would be the perfect opportunity to check the temperature gauge on her best friend's marriage.

"Any news on what's been going on with your crazy-ass wife?" Cassie asked John in a kidding, but serious way as the two friends caught up over drinks.

"Well, you're her best friend. I was banking on you for answers. I have tried everything," John said desperately. "She won't open up to me. She's as solid as Fort Knox."

"Do you think it's someone else?" Cassie asked gently, unable to make eye contact as she twirled the straw in her cocktail thinking of the Favorite Mistake.

"Wouldn't surprise me. She sure as hell wants nothing to do with me. She stiffens up when I try to touch her. She rarely looks me in the eyes when she tells me she loves me."

Cassie's heart hurt. Her mind flashed back to all of the memories she had of Liz raving about how John was her soulmate, how they were made for each other. A wave of bitterness filled Cassie's gut. This was a love that had started and grown right in front of her and was on the verge of dying.

As John and Cassie finished up their first round of cocktails, John's phone pinged. "It's Liz. They aren't going to make it back in time to meet us for dinner before her strict 9 o'clock bedtime. Guess we better go ahead and eat without them. We should probably order them some food, too. You know the dietary guidelines, Cas, so you do the honors." John handed her the menu and waved to the bartender. "We might as well be fully supportive spouses," John chuckled as he ordered two more bourbon and Cokes, following their dinner orders and Cassie's selection of two carryout pasta dinners. Time quickly got away from them as bourbon lightened the mood, and the conversation flowed easily over work and Kelly's acceptance of their job offer. Before they realized it, it was well past 9 o'clock. Aware of Rick's crucial need for a good night's sleep before a race, Cassie hugged John goodnight, nervous that she had stayed out too late to catch Rick before he fell asleep. But as she sheepishly entered her hotel room, toting cold pasta, Cassie was surprised to find that Rick wasn't back yet. Knowing that he had to leave at five a.m. for the race, she started to get worried. As she was undressing for bed, she heard the door creak open.

"Rick?" Cassie called, quickly grabbing the towel next to her suitcase to cover herself, confirming that it was in fact him and not a hotel attendant entering the wrong room.

"Hey, there," Rick said with a sexy growl, eyeing her towel-draped body. "I'm sorry we didn't make it to dinner. Liz is a mad woman. I'm so hungry and sleepy. I can't wait to wrestle in the sheets with you," he whispered, attempting to yank the towel away.

"It's way late and you have to save your energy for tomorrow," she said, slapping his hand away playfully. "You haven't even eaten yet. John and I brought back some dinner for you and Liz." Cassie pointed to the black plastic container sitting on the television stand, and then continued getting dressed for bed in her favorite silk pajamas.

"Well, I planned on being in bed an hour ago, but Liz wanted to go over the breathing and momentum chart one more time. She is so ridiculous. How have you dealt with her all these years?" Rick quizzed as he opened the plastic container and began inhaling the cold pasta. "If I don't die from exhaustion during the race tomorrow, I'm going to die of heartburn from eating this late. I hope you enjoy that hefty life insurance policy I have for you." Rick grabbed his chest and doubled over, mimicking a heart attack. Quickly Cassie's guilt for staying out late became overridden with annoyance for Liz's selfish demands.

"I'll make sure to have Tums and an energy drink on hand at the finish line," Cassie laughed, crawling into the cool sheets and watching Rick quickly shove bites of pasta into his mouth in between removing garments of clothing. A few minutes later, he was finally showered and settled for bed. As Rick snuggled close to her. Cassie smiled as she wrapped her legs tightly around his perfectly carved hips and buried her nose into the nape of his neck. She fought the selfish urge to ask him more questions about Liz's behavior tonight while they trained, knowing he needed his rest, and that the morning alarm would come way too soon.

The alarm clock blared at four thirty. Within ten minutes, Liz was pounding on the door. Rick was still in the bathroom getting ready, so Cassie begrudgingly inched out of the comfy hotel sheets to let her in.

"What the hell? He isn't ready yet?" Liz griped.

Before Cassie could answer, Rick opened the bathroom door and gave Liz a look from hell. "I told you I would meet you downstairs at four forty-five. Last time I checked, I still have five minutes to spare."

"I know. I'm just excited and nervous and so freaked out all at the same time," Liz said, jumping around and wringing her hands anxiously.

"You look like you are ready for a photoshoot, Liz, not a triathlon," Cassie looked puzzled at how much makeup and hair product her friend had on. Wasn't she going to be swimming in a lake and running and biking in the heat?

"When I look good, I feel good. And when I feel good, I perform well. Is there something wrong with that?" Liz defended, placing her hands on her hips.

"Guess not. But if there is a best dressed portion of the competition, you will win for certain," Cassie giggled shaking her head at her friend's strange behavior.

Rick leaned over and kissed Cassie on the cheek as he walked past her and out the door. Cassie caught a glimpse of an eye roll shooting from Liz's face and desperately fought the urge to slap the cynical smirk right off of it. Instead, she took the high road and gave Liz a high five.

"You can do this, Liz. You have it in the bag. And you have the hottest trainer out there." Cassie winked as she pinched Rick's firm backside, followed by a slap just to annoy Liz even more. "Go get 'em! John and I will see you at the finish line." The door shut behind them and Cassie breathed a sigh of relief.

Cassie crept back into bed, happy to get another hour and a half of sleep. She had been so exhausted lately and was hoping this time, that meant she was pregnant. It was so easy for her to read into every single possible symptom or sign like heartburn, fatigue, nausea, or any glimmer of hope that might prove this month would be the one.

———————

John and Cassie had made a plan at dinner the night before to meet at the coffee shop across the street from the hotel before heading to the race. She could smell the heavenly aroma of coffee before she opened the door and saw John's face.

"I took the liberty of ordering for you. Hope that's okay. After a hundred years of friendship, I know how you take your coffee." John handed her a warm to-go cup.

She smiled, taking a sip. "Perfection," she approved, giving him a thankful wink. "How was Cruella this morning? She made quite an entrance at my hotel door well before the rooster crowed."

"She was more like a rabid raccoon in my presence." Cassie laughed at John's accurate description as they headed to his car.

As they pulled into the parking lot at the race venue, Cassie noticed a text from Sarah. John almost crashed as she let out a level ten Publisher's Clearing House scream. "Oh, my goodness! They came?"

John slammed on the brakes from the outburst and looked at her with bugged eyes. "What? Who? Cas, seriously, I about wrecked the damn car!" he yelled, extremely agitated.

"Sorry," she said, looking at him apologetically with puppy dog eyes and a cute smile. "It's Sarah and Hal. They drove up from Savannah. They're waiting for us at the finish line."

"Really?" John's tune changed hearing the source of the excitement. "I didn't think they could come this weekend. I thought Sarah was on call after being off for the wedding and the honeymoon."

John barely had the car in park before Cassie slung open the door and made a mad dash for the finish line that would have rivaled the speed of any of the racers there that day. She spotted Sarah's blonde hair and Hal's bright white smile and nearly tackled them both.

"What? How? Yay!" Cassie was talking in tongues, making no sense at all as she kissed them both over and over on the cheeks. Sarah and Hal giggled like little kids being tickled while John was waiting patiently for the show to be over so he could hug Sarah too.

"Outta my way, you hog." John pushed Cassie off Sarah and managed a handshake with Hal at the same time. He picked up Sarah in a big bear hug and she gasped for air after he finally lowered her back to the ground.

"We wanted to surprise you," Hal beamed.

"Well, you nailed it." Cassie fist bumped the new groom. "Sarah, I thought you had to be on call this weekend?" Cassie couldn't take her eyes off how gorgeous and radiant Sarah looked. It was so great to see her so happy and in love. The glow looked good on her.

"I was able to switch with another doctor. How could I miss Liz's big race? How long ago did they start?"

Cassie looked down at her watch. "They should be about done, actually. We need to have our phones ready for some photo-finish pics. I can't wait to see her face when she crosses the line and sees you guys," Cassie squealed, leading Sarah closer toward the big blowup finish archway for the perfect view.

The official race time clock was nearing an hour and a half since the start. Rick usually finished around that time. He always opted to compete in the Clydesdale heat—for men over two hundred pounds. Cassie gave him such grief for competing in that category rather than his age group, but because he was tall and very muscular, he had the best chance at placing in that designation. He sure loved a shiny trophy and some bragging rights for his buddies, so he admitted he had no shame in entering the "big boy" class. It was hilarious to watch such a brawny, ripped man crossing the finish line in little short shorts next to all the "wafers," as he liked to call the runners that looked like tiny malnourished wind-up dolls whizzing by at the speed of light.

Within minutes, Cassie could see that Rick was rounding the last turn. The sweat covering his hard body highlighted each cut and crevice that moved with his every stride, while the bright sun reflected off his wet skin.

"There he is!" Sarah squealed as Cassie fumbled for her phone in her back pocket.

The four of them yelled loudly, cheering on his final stretch. "He heard us," Cassie confirmed as she watched him flash a cheesy grin despite his shortness of breath.

"Whoa! Look at the big guy finishing strong," yelled the emcee over the speakers as Rick crossed the line at a sprint.

Cassie ran over to give her Clydesdale a smooch on his sweaty lips. "Great job, babe."

"Got the energy drink and Tums?" he asked breathlessly, putting his hands on top of his head while flashing her a sexy wink.

"Can you believe Sarah and Hal are here?!" She turned around to see them smiling and snapping pictures. Despite his weak legs, Cassie watched as Rick made his way quickly over to their cheering squad.

John high-fived Rick right away and Hal gave his patented Southern gentleman firm handshake. Rick placed a breathless, sweaty kiss on top of Sarah's head and mumbled to her between gasps for air, "I thought you had to work, Doc."

"I couldn't miss Liz's first triathlon. Speaking of Liz, do you know how she's doing? Did you pass her on the course at all?" Sarah asked as she checked the time on the race clock.

"If I'm going by her training times, she should be finished in the next seven or eight minutes. I bet she finishes a little faster, though, because of the race day adrenaline," Rick predicted, checking who was rounding the corner to the finish line.

"What's she wearing so I can look out for her?" Sarah questioned. "I bet she spent days planning the perfect outfit for all of the race photos."

"But of course she did," John stated matter-of-factly in a mock British accent, giving a bow. "My lady must look perfect for the paparazzi. The princess herself chose to be adorned in a bright turquoise crop running top with turquoise camo bike shorts." John put one hand on his hip, casting his best fashionista sashay. They all laughed at the imitation and raw truth of Liz's husband's display.

"Oh, and don't forget full makeup and hair style to boot," Cassie added sarcastically as the turquoise outfit and tan skin came into sight. They all geared up their strongest vocals to cheer her on to the end. Liz looked amazing, and Cassie was filled with pride for her best friend, despite her being a huge pain in the ass lately.

"Go, Liz! Dig, dig, dig!" They all cheered words of motivation as she crossed the line, smiling from ear to ear. Rick and Liz embraced in a big, sweaty bear hug. Cassie smiled, knowing how proud Rick must have been, too, but she doubted he would sign up to train her again. It had probably taken more stamina for him to deal with her than it did for him to finish the race. Liz spotted Hal and Sarah and immediately started sobbing. She ran over to embrace them, drenching them in her sweat.

"What? How? I can't believe it! This means so much to me." Liz cried and laughed all at the same time while muttering her broken, breathless sentences.

"We wouldn't miss this for the world. You have worked so hard. We are so proud. We're going to celebrate big tonight." Sarah cheered and clapped, jumping up and down. The evening was sure to be filled with lots of catching up on the details of their honeymoon, and Cassie hoped to sneak some one-on-one time to fill in Sarah on Liz's new sexting hobby.

The Darling Oyster Bar had been on Cassie's "must do while visiting Charleston list," since spying an image posted on Instagram of the most gorgeous Bloody Mary she had ever seen. "Just wait until you guys see this drink. It's like its own little alcoholic meal. It's a huge glass of tomatoey concoction with not only a crab leg and claw sticking out of it, but a skewer with shrimp, olives, *and* a hush puppy," Cassie explained dramatically as they walked into the King Street venue. The heavenly smell of low-country oysters and salt filled the air. The long mahogany and marble bar didn't have a single vacant seat on that Saturday morning. The brick walls were irregular and perfect, making Cassie wonder how many voices had bounced off them over the hundreds of years since they were laid. The celadon leather looked inviting after the jaunt down King Street as they all crammed into one long booth.

"Aren't you glad now that I made you take the Epsom salt bath, Liz? Can you imagine how much sorer you would be?" Cassie asked, taking a big sip of The Captain, as the famous Bloody Mary was tagged. She had anticipated that Liz would complain all day about her aching muscles unless she did something to head off the problem, and she was determined to not let anything put a damper on the day.

"Yes. To you, Cassie Buchanon, I am forever indebted," Liz replied with a snarky smile.

"Here's to the most stylish and super-fly triathlete I know. May she never ever want to do this again and enlist me as her trainer." Rick raised his glass to Liz as she rolled her eyes, high-fiving her crab claw to his.

"Here's to the world's most hard-ass trainer. May he never have to yell at me or time me again. But I do appreciate all of it." Liz gave Rick a wink and took a sip. "Can we somehow recreate this gem back home? I could start every single non-workday with one of these babies." Liz pulled out the crab leg and started deconstructing it joint by joint with a precision that only a surgeon could display.

"Speaking of workdays, how is Kelly holding up by herself this weekend at the hospital?" Cassie asked, directing her gaze to Liz to see her reaction. "I can't believe she opted to stay the weekend and work for you guys while you were out of town. That was really kind of her."

"She is a go-getter, that's for sure. She signed the contract on Tuesday and asked, 'Where do you need me? I'm ready to start.'" John replied with an astonished tone. Liz's eyes were still focused intently on the crab leg and Cassie wondered if she even heard the conversation going on around her. "I haven't heard a peep from her yet, so I'm assuming everything is going okay. I told her to text me if she had any questions." John looked down at his phone to check for any missed messages. "None. Still all good.

But there is a text from Paul and Sam congratulating you on your race, Momma." John turned his phone toward Liz so that she could see the screen. Finally, her attention was drawn away from her drink. A big smile grew across her face, but Cassie could still see the wheels turning inside her friend's mind.

"Awe. My sweet babies. They really are the best kids ever," Liz said with an endearing tone and then reverted her focus back to the crab leg obviously avoiding the conversation.

"I am so thankful you're getting some help, Liz. You won't regret it. You will have so much more time for the boys and free time for yourself." Sarah grabbed Liz's hand, demanding her attention. "Where are the boys this weekend? I assumed they would be here to watch you race?"

"They are with my parents," John answered. "My dad wanted to take them fishing, and I thought it would be nice to have some adult time with my wife. I agree, Sarah. Once Liz wraps her head around the idea of having an associate, I think she will wonder why it took us so many years to hire one. Right, babe?" John pressed Liz.

"Um, yeah. It's gonna be great. She's great," Liz muttered, then shifted her attention right back to The Captain. John and Cassie made eye contact, noting Liz's dismissive response. The conversation quickly switched to Sarah and Hal's first few weeks in their new love world, and after another round of The Captains, the tipsy crew agreed to walk off some alcohol and keep Rick and Liz's muscles from moving into rigor mortis.

King Street was lined with brick pavers and eclectic boutiques. The old, cracked-walled buildings attested to a time long gone. And while they had been given face lifts with modern adornments and merchandise, the nostalgia of Charleston's history was still alive and present. As they strolled along the cobblestone streets with their maxed-out shopping bags, Cassie stopped to peep into the row of crisp art galleries filled with fine art and photography. One such gallery was filled with portrait photography. Families and children and tiny babies in their swaddles lined the walls and stood proud on easels. Cassie's heart sank. She had seen so many images like this on social media and had imagined what her photos would look like. She had designed every detail of her nursery in full detail, down to the sheets on the bed. As Rick stood behind her, she caught a view of his reflection in the glass window of the shop. Cassie knew he could read her mind.

"Cas," he whispered in her ear from behind as he wrapped his arms tightly around her shoulders. "It will happen soon enough. Trust me. Just enjoy the moment here with your friends." He planted a sweet kiss on her temple. Cassie knew he was right. She was due for her period any day now. The dread and anticipation were so familiar, and quite exhausting. She turned to him, giving him an acknowledging smile and kiss.

"Oh, Rick!" John squeaked in his most feminine and mocking voice as he watched Rick and Cassie's public display of affection, unaware of the sensitivity of their private conversation. "Take me now, you big hunk of a man!" He and Rick belted out with laughter as Rick gave two big, exaggerated pelvic thrusts into his wife. Cassie was thankful for her friend's uncanny ability to always make her laugh. She threw John a playful elbow to the gut behind her and he doubled over in fake pain. While John's acting display was horrific, his fake stomach injury did stir the crew's conversation for food. The calories from The Captains were long gone. They realized they had spent hours walking and shopping, while only making pit stops for cocktail refills in the pubs along the course of the day. Their buzzes from the drinks were as loud as the growls coming from their tummies.

They chose a nice steakhouse not far from their hotel. Substance in the form of meat, potatoes, and bread would be the only thing that would keep them standing after the long day of drinking they had enjoyed.

tink tink. John tapped his spoon to his wine glass to signal the group's attention. The red wine rippled inside the large vessel. As he raised his glass, Sarah quickly grabbed John's phone from the table beside her to capture the moment on video. As Sarah swiped up to enable video mode, a trail of texts popped up on the screen, all from Kelly. Liz's attention moved from her husband to his screen and to Sarah madly trying to close out the texts before he started his speech.

Just as John's first sentence began to roll off of his tongue, Liz pushed back from the table abruptly. "Fuck you, John! No one wants to hear your bullshit fluff." John's shell-shocked face told the truth. He had zero clue what bomb just went off inside of Liz's volatile mind.

"What are you talking about, Liz? Please sit down. You're making a scene," John hushed, looking around at the crowd of onlookers inside the restaurant. Liz grabbed the wine glass from his hand and threw the contents on his perfectly-tailored blue shirt and burst out of the black enamel-painted doors. Cassie innately jumped up to follow her, but not before seeing John with his pain, misunderstanding, and desperation to know why the one person he loved more than anyone would turn so hostile.

Cassie quickly caught the door as it nearly slammed closed in her face, and chased Liz out into the hot, humid night. She could see Liz, with her petite frame, leaning on the exterior of the building, her head hung and palms flat against the centuries-old brick. "What the actual fuck, Liz?" Cassie grabbed her arm, spinning her around to see Liz's tear-soaked face.

"I knew it!" Liz yelled, stomping her high heel onto the cobblestone.

"Knew what?" Cassie pleaded in utter frustration and oblivion.

"Kelly! John *and* Kelly! I knew this whole time it was a terrible idea to hire her." Despite hearing her words loud and clear, Cassie knew her face gave away her confusion. "When Sarah held up John's phone to video his lame toast, about a hundred text messages were on his screen from her."

"Liz, calm down. Did you see what they were about? She's on call for the first time alone in a brand-new hospital. He *did* tell her to contact him with any questions."

"No, but who cares? She knows he's here to celebrate *me* this weekend. Why would she think it was at all appropriate to message him that many times while he's off call and spending quality time with all of us? Surely, she can figure it out by herself. She's going to be the final nail in my marriage coffin *and* my business," she steamed, pacing back and forth on the sidewalk, wobbling in her heels from a combination of sore leg muscles, paired with way too much alcohol.

Cassie's mind went straight to Liz's Favorite Mistake. Somehow Cassie fought back the urge to slap the hypocritical demon out of Liz. Instead, she chose to comfort her, realizing that her pain must be stemming from a place she didn't have the ability to understand in that moment. Wrapping her arms around Liz, she pulled her in close. Liz melted into her as the tears fell from her cheeks onto Cassie's black silk camisole.

"Cas!" came Sarah's voice from the restaurant entrance. They locked eyes as Sarah spotted the two in an embrace. The men all filed out behind her while she shooed them away from the scene, pointing toward the hotel.

"Hal, we won't be long behind you," Sarah assured him. Cassie spotted John in his wine-soaked shirt. The shocked look on his face had turned to anger. Sarah wrapped her arms around her two friends as they crouched down together in unison to take a seat on the curb. With Liz supported tightly in between them, they sat there for a few minutes in silence, listening to Liz's whimpers.

Sarah brushed Liz's brown hair off her shoulder and whispered as only the sweetest, most loving pediatrician could do, "Liz, is there something you need to tell us?" How Cassie wished she had taken the time earlier in the day to tell Sarah about Favorite Mistake and his penis sexts. The day had been going so well, though, and she didn't want to ruin it. If Sarah had known about Liz's secret, she probably wouldn't have been so comforting and consoling.

"It's *her*. Kelly. I saw the texts pop up when you were recording. I *knew* hiring her as a partner would be the death of us. She's smart, beautiful, young, and now has constant access to my husband."

Sarah's eyes softened. "I thought that may have been what happened," she sighed as she looked at Cassie over Liz's shoulder, confirming her suspicions. "I took the liberty of asking John why Kelly was texting him like crazy. He let me read every single text message, Liz, and it was all about work. I promise. Someone was having complications from a surgery John had done on Wednesday and had to be admitted to the hospital. She was trying to get in touch with him. That's all."

Liz looked at Sarah with embarrassment and then buried her head in her hands. The sobbing got louder and louder, and Cassie knew they needed to get her back to the hotel. The three friends walked the five blocks, arm in arm, not speaking a word. As they stepped into the hotel lobby, Cassie ushered Liz over to a couch near the bar.

"Not another drink, Cas. That's the last thing we need," Sarah pleaded.

"No way. Water. And I think it would be best if we call John and talk to him before we take her to their room.

We have to make sure he's calmed down. Alcohol and anger don't mix well." Cassie pulled two barstools up to the bar within eyesight of Liz's couch, but out of earshot, and ordered three waters. She could see Liz was starting to nod off.

"We don't have much time before she passes out, so listen close. I have something to tell you about Liz. I will fill in the details later when we have more time. I wanted to tell you today, but I didn't have the chance." The heaviness in Cassie's voice alluded to Sarah this was something serious. Cassie glanced back one more time to check on Liz. She was still barely awake, and miraculously, hadn't puked yet.

"The other night when Rick and I had John, Kelly, and Liz over for dinner, Liz went to the bathroom and left her phone on my counter before everyone else had gotten there. I heard it pinging text message alerts, so I picked it up thinking it may be John. But hell no. It was a picture of a big hard dick." Sarah's eyes about popped out of her head at Cassie's words.

"Are you fucking kidding me?" Sarah exclaimed. Cassie shushed her and shook her head "no" with absolute certainty. "I'm assuming it wasn't John's penis by the way you're telling me this?" Sarah questioned.

"Well," Cassie confessed, "I haven't seen John's penis like *that* before, but let's just say that unless he is dying his hair down there, then no, it's not him."

"Well, who was it? Did you see who the message was from?"

"Yes. Kinda. His name is Favorite Mistake." Cassie tossed her a sarcastic, fake smile.

"Clever, of course. Liz is way too smart to have a real name saved in her phone for her secret sexter. Did you look to see the number? We have to figure this out," Sarah professed with determination.

"No, I was so rattled, I didn't think that quickly. I heard

her opening the door to the bathroom, so I had to scramble to put the phone back in its original place. I honestly didn't even really get a good close look at *it*." Cassie made a snarling face. "The picture was kind of blurry and I heard Rick coming in the back door at the same time."

"We're going to have to ask her who this guy is, Cassie."

"No, that's the last thing we need to do. You have been so busy with wedding stuff and you aren't around her in person like I am. Even John says she's in this weird, closed off, volatile space right now. She will never tell us. She will unfriend us before she divulges any information. I agree we have to intervene before John finds out and she loses everything that she adores in her life, but we need all the information first to see how best to handle the covert mission. Best case scenario is that she hasn't actually slept with this guy yet and it's only heavy flirting. That's a whole different ball game than a full-fledged affair."

Sarah and Cassie stared intently at each other, first with sadness, and then with a game face that only two best friends on a mission could do. John had answered Cassie's call and, after reluctantly hearing her plead Liz's case explaining the erroneous assumptions and reminding him that they were all way past the point of sobriety and making good decisions, he finally agreed to let Liz come to the room.

"Well?" Sarah asked as Cassie hung up the phone. "What did he say?"

"Not anything nice, unsurprisingly. I thought for a minute that we were going to have to get a separate room for the three of us. Let's see if we can get her back upstairs somehow," Cassie huffed as she saw that Liz had finally fallen asleep on the couch in the bar.

John was waiting with the door to their room cracked when they got off the elevator. He helped them toss

Liz's petite body onto the bed. The three of them started taking off her bra, earrings, and stilettos. Sarah laid Liz's clutch on the nightstand and brushed the hair from her face.

"Thanks, guys. I'm sure she won't remember a ton of details tomorrow, so will you go to bat for me? You know how stubborn she can be, and I'm sure she'll have a convoluted version of the accounts of the evening," John begged. They both promised to back him up and gave him their word that they would have a heavy conversation with Liz about her actions. He excused himself to the restroom while they finished tending to Liz, and as the bathroom door closed, Cassie's instincts took over.

"Sarah," she whispered with urgency, "grab Liz's phone out of her clutch."

"What?" Sarah looked at her confused, not following the orders.

"Just do it, damn it!" But Sarah just continued to look at her, not understanding her motive. "Move then. Hell, I'll get it." Cassie pushed past Sarah and fumbled open the clutch, her heart racing. She prayed she could pull this off before John came out from the bathroom. The phone thankfully still had charge. Liz was notorious for a dead phone battery. Well, at least that's what she had always claimed when her phone would frequently go straight to voicemail. Cassie wondered how legitimate that excuse had been, knowing about Favorite Mistake. Cassie quickly grabbed the limp hand that was hanging off the bed and pressed Liz's thumb to the home button, unlocking it.

"Cas, what are you doing?" Sarah hissed with shock.

"Hush, Sarah. Grab your camera." Sarah looked confused, but this time, she did as she was told. Cassie's fingers quickly went to Liz's contacts, scrolling down to the F's. And there it was: *Favorite Mistake*. Cassie nodded to Sarah and she took a quick picture of the number on the screen. They could hear John washing his hands and knew time was running out. Cassie quickly tapped into Liz's photos and swiped through them like a mad woman, trying to find any evidence of who this mystery man could be. Nothing unusual stood out. It was just the usual subjects—her, John, the kids, Cassie, Rick, Sarah, and Hal. But as luck would have it, she had saved the incriminating dick pic that Cassie had seen. She nodded to Sarah once again, and she quickly snapped a picture just as they heard John opening the door to the bathroom. Cassie tucked Liz's phone back into the clutch, and the two amateur investigators made their way to the door, bidding John farewell with hearts pounding.

Just as the elevator doors closed, Sarah burst out at the epic display of prying they had just pulled off. "What the heck made you think to do that?! Did you plan that?"

"No! I don't know what made me think to do that. I'm actually pretty impressed with myself." Cassie's voice was shaky from the adrenaline rush. "But when else would we be able to hack into her phone? I couldn't screenshot from her phone and text myself because she would see it."

"Your new nickname is Magnum P.I., Cas."

"Don't give me credit yet. We aren't done. We have more digging to do, but I guess his phone number and a picture of his hard cock is a good start. Shouldn't be too hard of a puzzle to put together, right?" Cassie said snarkily.

CHAPTER EIGHT

Cassie

S HE COULD FEEL the cool metal of the balcony rails pressing firmly into her back. Surprisingly, she wasn't scared at all, despite the long drop to the ground seven stories below. His arms were wrapped tightly around her, and her thighs were like a vice around his waist, pulling him in close. What should have been feeding her fear of heights actually instead ignited an exhilarating rush that made her entire body tingle. Her hands grabbed the back of his neck tightly as he pressed himself hard inside of her, sending a ripple of pleasure throughout her body. She felt completely safe, completely loved, and completely satisfied.

"Cassie," she heard him say her name, but the voice didn't match Dylan's face. "Cas!" She heard the voice even louder, as she was prematurely pulled away from the erotic scene, realizing it was instead Rick's voice, waking her frantically.

"What? Huh?" she answered out of sorts and a little foggy, probably from the leftover alcohol in her body. Praying that she hadn't been saying anything incriminating about Dylan in her sleep that Rick may have heard, she sat up quickly.

"Babe. Wake up. Look," Rick gasped, as she gazed down to see where he was pointing. Her vision was blurred, but even then, she could still see the cause of the frantic rousing.

"Oh, no," she whispered. There she was, sitting in sheets soaked with blood. It looked like a murder scene. Cassie stared at Rick in sheer horror. Her period was never heavy enough to cause that much bleeding. She rushed off to the bathroom, throwing her blood-drenched panties and favorite silk pajamas into the trash, knowing that they were ruined. As she started the shower and began to rinse, the realization that she once again wasn't pregnant overwhelmed her. It wasn't long before tears were streaming down her face, adding to the pink pool of water covering her feet. Cassie heard the shower curtain pull back as Rick climbed in with her, holding her tightly. But not even his embrace could console her anguish. Another month, another period, another disappointment, another wasted round of fertility meds, and another broken heart.

———◆———

The ride back home to Tampa was less than glorious. Rick had called Cassie's obstetrician, who was a colleague and friend of hers, to make sure she didn't need to be seen due to the excessive amount of bleeding. The doctor assured them that even if it had been a miscarriage, that it was way too early to need to do any other procedures. Cassie's body would handle it on its own, and he reminded them that it was normal in fertility treatments to have heavier bleeding, which was probably what had occurred. Still, the scene was unsettling, and neither Rick nor Cassie could get the vision out of their heads.

With the passenger seat reclined and her feet propped up on the dash, Cassie stared mindlessly out the window up toward the cloudy sky. The day before had been so sunny and gorgeous and fulfilling until Liz's outburst at dinner. It had since taken an ugly spiral downward. Cassie's heart was hollow, and her mind numb. She wanted desperately to believe in God's plan and timing for her, but disappointment and sadness made her doubt the whole process. The car stayed silent most of the way home, Rick's hand resting on her thigh. Cassie held a pillow over her stomach as her abdomen ached with some of the most agonizing cramps she had ever experienced. Not even pain medicine was touching the agony. She was in misery…plain and simple.

Cassie's mind shifted to Liz and John. She imagined that the car ride back for them would be a close second in the misery category, if not first place. She sighed a huge breath, signaling to Rick that she wasn't asleep, yet hinting at the start of a conversation that she wasn't one hundred percent sure she really wanted to have.

Rick turned his head to look at her, acknowledging her not-so-discrete proposition to break the silence. "Babe, I know you're upset, but it will happen eventually. You stressing so much is only making matters worse. Everyone says that, even the doctor." Rick squeezed the thigh he had been holding. Cassie turned to look at him, acknowledging his words. She knew he was right, but that was easier said than done.

"I know. It's just that Sarah is now married and well on her way to having a baby very soon, I'm sure, and I'm still here waiting for my turn, in last place."

"Cas, this isn't a race and it's definitely not something in our control. I know you're used to setting a goal and working hard to make it happen, but this isn't one of those things that works that way. This is the creation of another human. That's God's timing, not Cassie's."

Something about Rick's last comment seemed condescending, judgmental, and cruel. It sparked anger in her already-volatile soul. In retaliation and without even a moment's thought, she blurted out her best friend's secret to discount Rick's accusation of her excessive control over her destiny. "It's not fair!" she cried, pounding her fist into her hand. "And what about Liz? She doesn't deserve the blessed life she has. Not with what she's doing to John and her family. Not with her fucking *Mr. Favorite Mistake!*" Cassie's heart was racing, and she was just as shocked at her outburst of pent-up anger as Rick's expression told her he was.

"Favorite Mistake? Cassie, what are you talking about?"

Cassie gasped, trying to pull the words back into her mouth after she realized what she had said, but it was too late. Cassie groaned. She had already let the cat out of the bag, so she might as well go ahead with the details. Maybe he knew something that could help her and Sarah figure out the mystery man.

"Here. Look." She grabbed her phone, pulling up the evidence that she and Sarah had uncovered from Liz's phone the night before. As she flashed the screen toward Rick, his face went stone cold and white.

"Where did you get that picture?" Rick asked, his voice sounding uneasy. He stared at the image of the man's erect penis in all of its glory long enough for Cassie to feel slightly uncomfortable at his interest in another man's parts.

"Well, the original time I saw it was when John, Liz, and Kelly came over for dinner the other night. Liz was in the bathroom and her text alert went off. I figured it was John, so I picked up her phone. And this is obviously *not* John," Cassie muttered, zooming in on the dark hairs and flashing the image toward Rick. He slapped his hand over his eyes to block the inappropriate zoomed-in image. "When Liz was passed out last night, Sarah and I were able to get the pictures off her phone. We were totally impressed at our investigative skills," she bragged proudly, despite the seriousness of the subject. "We have to find out who this guy is so we can stop this trainwreck before John finds out and it ruins her life."

Rick stared straight ahead at the road and made no eye contact as he spoke to his wife. "What do you all know about this guy? Are you sure it's an actual affair and not just some heavy flirting?"

"We don't know anything but what I have told you, and I'm sure Liz won't tell us who it is. We got his phone number, too, but obviously haven't tried calling it yet or tracing it. This morning has been quite eventful, so Liz's promiscuity has taken a backseat." She glanced down at the numbers of the contact information. "I don't recognize the number, but that's no shocker. Who even remembers phone numbers these days with cell phones and contact lists? Do you know anything, Rick? You spent quite a lot of time training her recently. Did she ever mention anyone or did anyone else ever show up to meet her?"

"No, never," Rick denied, still focusing intently on the highway. "She was so fierce in her workouts that it didn't leave much room for conversation. Time has a way of working things out, Cassie. I'm sure that whatever is happening with Liz and John and this mystery man will eventually settle. You're an amazing friend to Liz. Trust me, I've come to realize this even more over the past few months. Liz is fun and has an amazing heart, but she can be selfish and needy. You and Sarah always come to her rescue. Sometimes you have to let people fight their own battles. Don't pry too much into her situation. Let her figure this one out on her own. You need to stay focused on *our* family. Adding her stress to your plate won't help."

"I don't know, Rick. I'm not sure she can fix this by herself. She's a fucking mess," she huffed in despair. "But for our sake, you're probably right. Maybe for once, I should let Liz get herself out of the big-ass hole she's dug." Smiling at him, she squeezed Rick's hand in reassurance. The sun was coming out from behind the clouds and warming her skin through the car window. She felt slightly relieved from the pressure she had put on herself to solve Liz's life problems. She vowed to put her focus back onto her own marriage and maybe all the other pieces would fall into place. Hopefully they would, anyway.

CHAPTER NINE

Liz

LIZ'S HEAD POUNDED. The hangover was brutal. Her mind raced and her heart sank with thoughts of last night's events. She had slept most of the way home from Charleston, partly because of her hangover and partly to separate herself from the awkward silence in the car. She was sure John had nothing kind or productive to say. *Where have I gone wrong? When did my life take such an ugly turn?* But truthfully, she knew the answer: Rick. Her mind shifted to last Monday. She'd known it was Cassie's day in the OR and John was busy interviewing Kelly, so she'd taken Rick up on his offer.

"Come over at lunch. We'll have the house to ourselves. Please, I can't keep my mind off you." Rick begged to Liz over the phone. "Trust me, no one will know. Pull into the garage. I'll open the door for you."

She could still remember the feel of the sheets. They were so cool and crisp against her skin. His warm body against hers, the heat of his breath against her neck, and the sound of his voice in her ear sent chills down her spine. They laid there, in her best friend's bed, naked, hearts still pounding from their lovemaking until the post-orgasm rush wore off and Liz's mind became overwhelmed with guilt.

"I need to go," she whispered quickly.

"Why? What's wrong?" Rick asked, shocked at her abrupt change of tone.

"Oh, nothing. I just need to get back to the office. I'm sure John will bring Kelly by and wonder where I am. I can only use the excuse of making rounds for so long," she assured him, knowing that what she really wanted to do was be alone and somehow stop her mind from racing.

As she sat in her car at a stoplight on her way back to the hospital, tears had streamed down her face. Liz glared at her hands that tightly gripped the steering wheel. She blared the radio to try and drown out the sound of her sobs, but to no avail. Her diamond wedding ring stood up high like the Hope Diamond, casting a kaleidoscope rainbow reflection onto the interior of her car. Her eyes closed, causing her lids to dump even more tears down her cheeks. Her heart ached with guilt thinking of where she had just been... but he felt so good. How could something so wrong fulfill her every need? Or maybe it was a want? How could she feel this way about another man? John had once held her soul in the palm of his hand. What was left of that grip seemed to be sliding through his fingers. It wasn't from a lack of him trying. If anyone deserved a "husband of the year" award, it was John. There wasn't a box he hadn't checked on her "perfect man" list. For years, he had been her best friend, her soulmate, her confidant, and her business partner. And somehow, in a short moment of weakness and vulnerability, she had let someone else in. It was the biggest mistake she had made in her life to date. But there was something about Rick that made her feel so alive again. Something that ignited a fire she was once was known for. *Even in the most perfect marriages, there was always a longing for more, right?* whispered a little voice of doubt that couldn't be snuffed out. *Am I still attractive to other men? Does every man see me simply as a married mom of two boys?* Since her affair with Rick had began, Liz felt sexy, sensual, irresistible, and feminine. The first time he'd looked into her sad eyes, she'd known she wouldn't have the strength to resist him. The first time he'd brushed the hair out of her face, her heart stopped. And the first time he'd kissed her lips, she'd thought she might die if she never felt him inside of her.

But now it was all coming to a head. Paranoia had taken over her mind and was now spilling out uncontrollably for the rest of the world to see. Somehow, she had to make it all stop.

John had been kind enough to carry in all their luggage and set it in the mudroom, just like every other trip that they had taken over the years. The thought had crossed Liz's mind that he might not take his suitcase out of the car. She wouldn't blame him if he dropped her off and kept going. She had some major apologizing to do, but she couldn't think of where to start and her pounding head hurt way too much to even try to use it for coming up with meaningful words. She pulled out the plastic dirty laundry bag from John's suitcase to start the washer, just like she always did at the end of every trip over the years. But this time, as the bag emptied into the washer, she wasn't greeted with the sweet scent of his cologne, but rather with the stench of alcohol. There it was, staring back at her like a murder weapon, was the wine-soaked shirt from the previous night. With it cradled in her hands, tears streamed down her cheeks.

John didn't deserve what she was doing to him. All he had ever done was love her wholly. Liz's feet couldn't take her to find him fast enough. There, in the room where they had loved so many times, stood her husband. She stood in the doorway, unable to control her crying, knowing John could hear her behind him. She knew his heart must be so full of pain and anger and questions.

"What, Liz?" he asked, not turning around, blatantly unapathetic to her breakdown.

"I'm sorry. I'm so, so sorry." Liz barely got the words

out between heaves and cries as she held on tightly to the wine-soaked shirt. She stood there shaking and vulnerable, hoping that he wouldn't ignore her plea for forgiveness. Even though he had every right to.

"I know, Lizzie." John finally whispered after an awkward moment of silence. As he turned and made eye contact, his look of defeat revealed that he was caving to her plea, despite his intended toughness. Liz melted into him as he went to her, wrapping his arms tightly around her petite body. She knew her apology wasn't just for last night, but she didn't have the courage or the strength yet to fully come clean. Their struggle wasn't over, but this was a good start. As she looked up at him with her big blue, tear-drenched eyes, he leaned down and kissed her softly, gently, completely acknowledging her fragility.

John swept her up in his arms and laid her carefully down on the Egyptian cotton sheets of their nest. As he crawled on top of her, Liz stared tenderly into his loving eyes. Her hand touched his chest to feel his pounding heart. *That heart.* The heart that was so big, so forgiving, so safe, and had been given entirely to her so many years ago. It was precious. How could she have been so unfaithful, so careless with it? As remorse welled up inside of her, she buried her face in his neck and let him take control. He navigated his hand up her back with precision, unlocking her bra with one hand. His familiar moves put her at ease, and she let go. She let his arms, his body, his soul, engulf her inside and out. And for the first time in months, she made love to her husband. There was no raw passion, no hairpulling, no crazy venues. Just slow, passionate love. The kind where no words need to be spoken. John curled up behind her as she lay peaceful on her side, his body limp with pleasure. Her gaze fell upon their bedside table. There, in black and white, was their wedding portrait staring back at her. That day had been a fairytale. She had promised to love him forever and only him.

Liz felt nauseous. Only days ago, she had lay this same way with another man. She had smelled him, touched him, loved him the way she had promised she would only do with John. The photo turned blurry from her tears. John was breathing heavy, signaling that he had fallen fast asleep. Liz knew what she had to do. As she slowly snuck out of the warm bed, she couldn't help but notice how sore her bare feet were as they touched the floor. Yesterday's race and the high heels of the evening were coming back to haunt her. She slipped quickly into the soft pink robe their two sons had given her last Christmas and tiptoed into the kitchen to find her phone. Grabbing it with shaky and unsteady hands, she typed the words she knew she must say.

I can't do this anymore. I'm drowning.

She hit the send button quickly, so as not to change her mind. As much as she was wracked with guilt, she really did love her forbidden fruit. Even if it was lust or infatuation, he made her feel alive and sexy and powerful. But just as important to her was their friendship that she knew would never be the same. She was destined for a heartbreak either way, whether it be from John, *him*, or both.

Ping. His response was too quick and too short, she thought, before reading it.

Me too. I agree.

Her stomach dropped and her heart broke into a million pieces on the kitchen floor. And just like that, heartbreak was ignited. *He didn't even put up a fight*, she thought to herself. Her gut churned. She felt cheap and used. Had this all been a game to him? How could he have been so quick to let her go? After all, he had told her he loved her. He had made love to her in more places and positions over the past few months than she could count. As she threw her phone back into her bag, she fell to the floor and lay there, staring at the smooth, white kitchen ceiling, crying tears of confusion and shame, swirled together into a heap of pain.

CHAPTER TEN

Cassie

THE WHEELS OF the hospital gurneys traveling down the long hall of the surgical floor whistled annoyingly. Cassie should be immune to the sound, but it was another Monday, and, in that moment, all of her senses were on full alert. Everything was irritating her, from the slowpoke car she had gotten behind on the way to work, to the giggling women at the nurse's station. No amount of CBD, ashwagandha, or kava kava could have simmered her down. She couldn't blame it on hormones. After the incident in Charleston two weeks ago, Cassie and Rick had decided it may be best to give her body a break from the fertility medications for a month or two. But truthfully, it was their marriage that needed a break from the stress more than anything. Cassie's baby agenda had taken over their lives and it was starting to take a toll on them physically, mentally, and intimately. Rick had been cold since their return from the Charleston trip. She could feel him pulling away. He had barely touched her. His office had been his hideaway, and it was clear that Cassie wasn't invited into it.

She tried with every inch of her being to focus on finishing her surgical notes for the morning. Her stomach growled with hunger for lunch, and her lungs ached for some fresh air from the smothering concrete walls closing in on her. Just as she was typing her last note, she heard a low female voice behind her.

"Cassie?" She turned to see the gorgeous, tall blonde that was unintentionally wreaking havoc on her best friend's marriage.

"Oh, hey, Kelly. I was concentrating on these surgical notes from this morning. Sorry I didn't hear you."

"No, I don't mean to disturb you at all, but I wanted to make sure John is okay. He's seemed sort of distant to me, and I didn't know if he had mentioned anything that could be bothering him. I really want our partnership to work out, so I don't want to sweep anything under the rug that I may be doing wrong."

"Kelly, Charleston was exhausting in so many ways." Cassie's mind flashed back to the emotional plummet the trip had caused in conjunction with massive hangovers. "I'm sure John is just tired and still catching up from last weekend. He was so at ease knowing you were taking calls for him. He adores you and has full confidence in you." She smiled at Kelly, despite the small, undisclosed bit of information that she had ruined their trip with her emergency texts. There was no way Cassie was about to put that kind of guilt on the poor girl's shoulders.

"Really? Thanks for telling me that. Liz has been a little tough to read and standoffish, but John has been nothing but amazing during this whole process. That's why it concerned me when his demeanor did a one-eighty. I'll leave you to your notes. So sorry to get you off track. Let's do dinner again sometime soon, okay?"

"Sure thing. I would love to." As the tall Barbie doll doctor coasted gracefully down the hall, Cassie's resentment toward Liz amplified. Kelly was a godsend for their practice. Hopefully, Liz wouldn't be using the extra time away from the office to maximize on her rendezvous with her Favorite Mistake. That, for sure, would be counterproductive. Which reminded Cassie that she needed to follow up with Sarah on tracing the cell number they'd heisted from Liz's phone. Yet another distraction. Cassie grabbed her cell from her white lab coat pocket and scrolled down her favorites list to find Sarah's number. As she hit the call button, Cassie immediately morphed into investigator mode as she scanned the area to see who might overhear her conversation. But not surprisingly, there was no answer.

"She's probably alligator wrestling a toddler," Cassie muttered to herself. Instead of leaving a voicemail that Sarah may not get as quickly, she opted to shoot her a text.

Any info on Project P.I.?

She and Sarah had decided on a code name for uncovering the mystery man, paying homage to *Magnum P.I.* by coining their agenda *Mission: Penis Identification*. Cassie chuckled at the clever absurdity and inappropriateness of the code name, despite it being anything but a laughing matter.

Cassie managed to finish her surgery notes while waiting for Sarah's reply. She realized she should have done dictation in her private office to separate herself from the distractions, but she would have been off-key there too. The walls and shelves had become adorned with pieces of the past and images of her dearest people. It had been her home away from home since starting at Tampa Regional. She couldn't possibly count the hours she had spent sleeping on the tan leather couch during on-call rotations. Where the space had once been her sanctuary, it had become too heavy emotionally. Recently, pictures of Liz and John made her heart ache. The bowl of seashells from Sarah's wedding reminded her of being hours away from her and how badly she needed her there. The picture of her and Rick on the steps of their house on the day they'd moved in poured salt into her open wounds. They had hoped to fill that home with the pitter-patter of tiny feet and babies' cries that still didn't exist. It seemed the whole room had been invaded by a dense fog that smothered her and opening a window to let the fresh air in wouldn't help.

Cassie could feel her pocket vibrate as she pushed through the double doors to exit the hospital. It was a beautiful Florida day. The breeze blew through the palms, making a slapping sound reminiscent of the beach. The sun shone brightly, causing Cassie squint to read the reply text from Sarah that had finally come through.

Call you in five.

Since it was such a gorgeous day, Cassie decided on an outdoor venue for lunch while she waited on Sarah's call. And it would give her some privacy outside the hospital walls to talk candidly to Sarah. Spying eyes and prying ears were always creeping around the hospital. The social dynamics and cliques of doctors and staff were well known, and there was nothing more coveted in the healthcare scene than a good scandal. Cassie's worst nightmare would be someone putting together the pieces of her conversation with Sarah. She wasn't sure which would be scarier: a leaked partial version of the story or the actual whole story. She was unpacking her lunch, perched in the shade on a park bench when Sarah called.

"Hey, lady. How many kids have you scarred for life today?" Cassie teased.

"Funny, Cas. No time for jokes. Gotta make this quick. I'm headed in for some rounds on the maternity floor," Sarah said in a short tone. "Here's the scoop. I have tried calling the number several times. Obviously, I got no answer, and no voicemail is set up with a name or anything. I traced it, trying to see who owned the number, but it's a burner. Whoever it is obviously doesn't want his wife or girlfriend to know about Liz either. Looks like we're out of luck for now until we get some more info."

"Shit. It's weird that Liz wouldn't have gotten a burner too. Maybe she doesn't care if John finds out, but I can't imagine her wanting to hurt him like that. This whole situation is so out of character for her. Do you think she has a brain tumor?"

"I doubt it. Sounds more like a mid-life crisis. But I gotta go. Love you."

"Love you too."

By the time she finished eating, the sun had made its way around the shade tree and was hitting Cassie square in the face. But she didn't mind. It felt good. She wasn't sure if it was the warmth of the sun or the energy from its rays that seemed to recharge her, but instantly a sense of peace and reassurance that all of this craziness was going to end soon and it would all be okay came over her. She was pressed with the need to see her husband. It was almost a panicky, sixth sense-type feeling, similar to when you feel like someone you love may have just been in a car crash or a mass shooting. It was that immediate need to hear their voice or see them to make sure they were safe and sound. She missed him. She missed his touch and his warmth. In that instant, she knew what she needed to do. She wasn't sure what empowered her, but she picked up her phone and dialed the number to her office.

"What's up, doc?" Tara, the patient scheduler, answered, giggling at the *Looney Tunes* reference, obviously taking advantage of caller ID.

"Clever, Tara," Cassie responded, shaking her head unamused. "Nothing's wrong, but I need you to cancel my afternoon. I'm not sick, but I have something I need to take care of. I'll be back in the morning." Cassie hung up before Tara could dig any further. She smiled, feeling so liberated. She had never played hooky from work in all her years in practice. Cassie took her job and her patients' time very seriously, but she decided to put her marriage first. Rick was at home working, and a good sexy surprise and afternoon of lovemaking was just what the doctor ordered to rekindle their flame.

CHAPTER ELEVEN

Liz

LIZ HAD BEEN beside herself for days. She hadn't eaten or slept. She wasn't sure if it was from the guilt she was feeling about what she had done to John over the past few months, or from the gut-wrenching sadness of terribly missing the man she knew she shouldn't love. She hadn't heard a peep from Rick since she'd ended their relationship via text. The fact that he hadn't argued with her or tried to make her change her mind drove her crazy. Well, crazier. Her heart was ripped wide open. She had to stop the bleeding somehow. She grabbed the only tourniquet she had in her possession: her car keys. Before she had time to think about what she was doing, she found herself knocking on his front door. She wasn't sure what possessed her, or what made her think this was any sort of a good idea, but it was the last tool in her toolkit, her Hail Mary.

When Rick opened the door, her heart sank, and tears filled her eyes at the sight of him. She didn't know who was more surprised that she was so boldly standing there at the front door of his home in broad daylight unannounced, her or him.

"Liz. What are you doing here?" He peeked around the door to make sure no one was around.

"I don't know. I miss you." She sounded pathetic and her words quivered as they exited her mouth.

"Come in. No one needs to see you here. Where did

you park?"

"Around the corner. Don't be silly. I'm just as scared of getting caught as you are." Liz huffed. He was a mess too. She could tell from his puffy eyes and baggy white T-shirt that he hadn't slept well or eaten much either.

"Liz, we can't do this anymore. We have to stop. Cassie and Sarah know you're having an affair." Rick paced as he ran his fingers anxiously through his already messy dark hair.

"What? How do you know? What did Cassie say?"

"I'm not sure exactly how, but when you were passed out in Charleston, they got into your phone and got my burner number. Cassie had seen the picture I sent you on my way home from the airport before dinner the other night. I guess you were in the bathroom and she saw the text or something, so she and Sarah decided to try and get the name of the *Favorite Mistake*, knowing you wouldn't give them any information. Clever name, by the way. You never mentioned that to me. Thank God you didn't have it saved under my real name." Rick rolled his eyes, annoyed. "I should have insisted you get a burner too. I don't know why I didn't press you further on that." Rick slapped his forehead in stupidity.

"Me having an extra phone lying around for Paul or Sam to get ahold of while digging in my purse for gum or cash for the vending machine was bound to be more noticeable and draw way more attention than the risk of someone seeing your dick pop up on my phone."

"Okay, whatever. That's obviously a moot point now," Rick said despite still being annoyed. "Anyway, Sarah has been calling the burner, I guess trying to see if there was a voicemail, or better yet, if someone would answer. I have had tons of missed calls on it from her cell number and from what I'm assuming is her office number. It's a matter of time before they dig deeper." Rick buried his face in his hands.

"How did we get ourselves into this?" Liz asked, defeated. "Well, at least I know now why you were so quick to quit on me, on us. After you didn't ask any questions or try to make me change my mind when I texted you, I was feeling like a used piece of trash. I felt so cheap, like the cheating wife that I am." Liz's eyes dumped guilty tears down her cheeks.

"You know that isn't the case. You know how I feel about you. It's just too hard. We have good lives with good people that we love. To destroy them would be a death sentence for both of us." He grabbed her, wrapping his arms tightly around her petite frame. She touched his chest and her heart started to race. He had that sort of electrical power over her. His hand stroked her cheek and wiped away the tears as they streamed down her face. He kissed the top of her head like he always had to reassure her and grabbed her hair tightly between his fingers. He whispered in her ear, "I miss you."

As she looked up at him, she saw the face of a man she loved, but knew she could never possess. But at least she did in that moment. "I miss you more," she whispered.

In one swift motion, he had her in his arms and in his bed. She couldn't get to his skin fast enough. Every stitch of clothing was but a roadblock. She climbed on top of him and, clutching his hands tightly in hers, she kissed him over and over again, not knowing if it would be their final kiss. Somehow, he managed to break one hand free from her tight grip and grabbed her hip as he pushed himself inside of her. Liz gasped at the sensation. Chills ran down her spine as they made love, slow and intentionally.

CHAPTER TWELVE

Cassie

CASSIE HAD PULLED into her driveway a thousand times before, but this time was different. Her heart raced with excitement at the thought of surprising Rick. It was so out of character for her. Cassie didn't have a spontaneous bone in her body, having been pegged as the calculated and predictable one. Rick needed to see this side of her. For months, she had timed and micromanaged every aspect of their lovemaking—or better yet, baby-making. She had stressed and analyzed their intimacy so much that it had become a job rather than pleasure. He was slipping away, and she had no one to blame but herself. Hopefully, this effort would reset their bond and they could get back to good.

Quietly, Cassie crept into the house, slipping her shoes off by the back door as she started unbuttoning her blouse. Her heart was pounding with excitement to see Rick's reaction. Layer by layer, she dropped pieces of clothing onto the warm birch floors as she tiptoed her way through their home. She peeked into his office, expecting to see him sitting there at his desk, but the room was empty. His computer screen still showed his work, so he hadn't been up from his desk long enough to invoke the sleep screen. Cassie giggled with child-like excitement as she heard him rustling around in their bedroom. She was like a kid sneaking to catch a glimpse of Santa. She couldn't wait to see the look on his face…

But as she rounded the corner to the doorway of their bedroom, having made it down to only her bra and panties, Cassie saw something she would never be able to unsee. Her heart stopped. Her breathing stopped. Her world stopped. There, in her bed, was her husband and her best friend.

"Cassie!" Rick yelled, seeing her standing in the doorway, frozen, as he peered past Liz's shoulder. Liz gasped as she jumped off Rick and covered herself with Cassie's sheets.

Cassie just stood there, paralyzed, not speaking a word. As they both scrambled to get their clothes on, Cassie didn't move. She couldn't. She stood in silence, practically naked, staring at them. She felt faint, like someone had stabbed her and the blood was pouring from her veins and pooling at her feet. Rick and Liz swirled around her in slow motion, muttering words that only sounded like the roar of a subway, gathering what was left of their integrity, and their clothes. It was like watching a horrific accident happen right in front of her. She wanted to hit the rewind button, scream and make it stop, but she had no control and no strength to fight the moment. She turned like a zombie and headed toward the garage, with no other gut intuition but to get as far away from them as she could. Before she knew it, she was sitting in her car, half naked, driving to the only place where she knew she would feel safe: Bayshore Drive.

She parked her car facing the dark blue bay, not sure what was stopping her from racing it straight into the waves. She wanted to. Instead, she sat in the driver's seat in silence, trying to digest all that had slapped her in the face. Suddenly, everything started to become clear as the past few months swirled in her head. The training hours spent together were an easy alibi. Rick's distance since she had confided in him about Liz's Favorite Mistake now made sense. And probably the deepest cut was Rick dumping all his sperm into her best friend as she tried desperately to get pregnant.

And then there was Liz, her best friend, the one who stood by her side at her wedding. The one that had consoled her when her had heart broken into a million pieces over lost love and lost dreams. The one that had reassured her that life was hard, but precious, had ultimately been the one who had shown her how brutally unfair life could be. Liz hadn't just been killing her relationship with John; she had killed theirs too.

Cassie stared out at the rippling water of the bay, wanting to jump in and keep swimming and swimming, maybe even be engulfed by the water. Instead, she reached into her purse and grabbed her phone.

Tara answered once again, "What's up—"

Cassie cut her off in midsentence to spare herself the joke and Tara the danger of what Cassie might do to a person with a smart-ass comment at that moment. "Turns out I am sick. Please reschedule my books for the rest of the week. I'll let you know when I'll be back. I'm okay, but you may not be able to get me for a few days." She hung up before Tara could ask any questions.

Next, she dialed Sarah, and this time she answered. Stating only minimal facts and few details, she hung up the phone and headed north to Savannah. The next five hours were a blur of palm trees that turned into tall Georgia pines. As she walked up to Sarah's door in panties and the Rolling Stones t-shirt that she had quickly grabbed from the laundry room during her panicked exit, she didn't even have to knock. The door swung open as Sarah pulled her into her arms and Cassie collapsed. There were no words, just tight hugs and sobs. They sat on her gray velvet couch for what seemed like hours in silence. With Cassie's head in Sarah's lap, she stroked Cassie's hair like she could only imagine Sarah had done so many times to her sweet, sick children. Now, Cassie was the patient and so grateful for her friend's God-given gift of comforting the weak. Cassie didn't have the courage to speak. If she said something, anything, it might confirm the reality that this wasn't a bad dream. She would be conceding to her new shit show of a life. It took Sarah bringing back two highball glasses filled with a stout Kentucky bourbon to get words to exit her mouth.

"You don't have to say anything if you don't want to. We can sit here for days if that's what you need," Sarah reassured, placing her hand on Cassie's naked thigh.

"How could they?" Cassie squeaked out. It took the throat-numbing power of the bourbon to get the painful words out.

Sarah shook her head and looked down at her hands in remorse. "I don't know. But I do know one thing: whatever the 'why' is has nothing to do with you or anything you did to deserve this pain. I feel so stupid that I didn't pick up on it. I am the best friend of both of you. How did I get so out of touch?" Sarah shook her head in disbelief. This time, even the miracle worker herself couldn't fix this disaster.

Reality started to set in as Cassie looked down at what she was wearing. A ratty old Rolling Stones tee and a pair of black panties.

"Look at me." Cassie started laughing hysterically. It was a true crazy laugh. Like one a certified lunatic would belt out. Sarah followed suit. "Can you believe I drove all the way here to Savannah in this? Thank goodness I didn't get pulled over."

"I certainly hope you didn't make any pit stops for gas or bathroom breaks," Sarah chuckled, throwing her hands over her eyes in embarrassment.

"Honestly, who knows. I may have. I don't even remember the drive here. But I'm sure if I did, we will see footage on social media any moment." After the crazy belly laughing stopped, a somber wave rushed over Cassie's face as the image that will forever be burned into her mind resurfaced vividly.

"I cannot express how crippled I became when I saw them together, Sarah. It was like someone punched me in the gut so hard it knocked the breath out of me. I saw Liz's back moving on top of Rick. I saw his hands on her ass, grabbing her firmly and pressing her down onto him." Cassie paused, trying to keep the bile in her stomach contained. "It had to be a good ten seconds before they noticed me, which doesn't seem that long, but is an eternity when you're watching your best friend fuck your husband. And the noises, the breathing, the sheets rustling. It's still ringing in my ears." She closed her eyes and tears rolled like bowling balls, heavily spinning down her cheek.

Cassie's eyes popped open. "Do you think John knows? Should I tell him, or let her?" Cassie panicked thinking of John's reaction to the situation.

"John knows," Sarah sighed. "He called me just before you got here."

"I'm assuming you haven't heard from Liz yet. I doubt she is ready to face the wrath of your scolding." John's pain had to be as great, if not greater than her own. "What did John say? How is he?"

"He was pitiful. But do you know that in all his pain, his main concern was you? He wanted to call you and make sure you were okay. I told him it was best to give you some space and you would call him when you were ready. I texted him when you got here, and I could almost hear a sigh of relief through his response." Sarah smiled and chuckled at his typical big brother-like response. How many times had he put to rest their fears and sorrows? From breakups to bombed tests to infertility, John had been there to console them. Cassie could feel the bourbon making her lips numb and her head light. She realized she hadn't eaten since lunch in the park, when she'd decided to make a surprise midday visit home. And what a surprise it had turned out to be. She couldn't stomach anything to eat but she definitely didn't need to drink anymore.

"I think I want to go to bed now."

"Your favorite bed is waiting on you. Sheets are pulled back, ready for you to slide into, sweet girl. If you need anything, let me know. Hal has to be on call at the hospital tonight, so he won't be in until tomorrow morning. Do you want me to sleep with you?" Cassie shook her head despite Sarah's kind gesture. She wanted to be alone and wallow around in the sheets by herself.

Sarah's bed from med school was Cassie's favorite. As roommates, the three girls had spent hours with papers spread out all over it, studying for their next big exam, and even more hours laying on it, laughing and crying and trying to figure out life and boys. When Sarah had been gone, Cassie would sneak naps in it and sometimes even sleep with Sarah at night when Dylan wasn't staying at their apartment. It was the best mix of soft and firm, cool and warm, crisp and cozy. But the real truth was that it felt safe.

Cassie had threatened to disown Sarah if she ever got rid of it. She had even offered to buy it from her on multiple occasions. Sarah had promised to keep it as a guest bed, ready for Cassie to crawl into anytime, and so far, she had held true to that promise. Cassie barely remembered sliding in between the sheets…

———◆———

The smell of cinnamon crept into the room like a wave of deliciousness. Cassie assumed Sarah was up and making her favorite breakfast: cinnamon rolls and bacon. Even with the heavenly feel of the bed and the smell of comfort foods, she had to blink a few times to take in the view and remember where she was. Yesterday, unfor-

tunately, hadn't been a bad dream. She stared out the
second story windows that were adorned with tropical
bamboo shades. She could see the tops of palm trees and
Spanish moss in the live oaks blowing in the morning
breeze. It was so calming. The sky was blue with bright
white clouds speckled across it. Sarah's voice was coming
from the kitchen, and Cassie assumed she was talking to
Hal, but realized the tone was too angry for it to be him.
Sarah and Hal had never so much as raised a voice at each
other, much less argued. Cassie stepped quietly out of the
bed and walked to the edge of the stairs where she could
clearly hear Sarah's voice swirling up the stairwell. Peeking around the corner slowly as she stood quietly on the
last step, she saw Sarah's back to her. With her phone in
one hand and the other hand pointing angrily in thin air
toward an invisible target, Cassie knew who Sarah must
be talking to.

"You have no right! What you have done is unspeak-
able on so many levels. Have you any idea how many
lives you've hurt? Or do you even care? Right now, the
best thing you can do is to try and mend your marriage. Cassie is *not* your concern and if she ever wants
to give you a chance to plead your case, you will be the
first to know." Cassie watched silently as Sarah hung up
and slammed her fist down onto the counter, clearly trying to compose herself after ending the call. Cassie was
flabbergasted. She had never heard Sarah yell at anyone
like that before. Cassie's heart sank, knowing the turmoil
their trio was in. She wasn't quite ready to dive into the
details of the phone conversation just yet, so she quickly
and quietly scurried back into the bed, hoping not to be
caught listening in on Sarah's conversation with Liz. The
sound of steps and smell of cinnamon, coffee, and bacon
were drawing nearer. Cassie rolled over unsuspiciously to
see Sarah carrying a large tray.

"Breakfast in bed, my sweet lady," Sarah said cheerfully,

setting the tray down over her friend's lap. She had successfully shed her anger and put on a happy face with the skills of a well-trained actress.

"You may never get me to leave. I'm starving."

"How did you sleep? Were you able to get any rest?" Sarah asked softly.

"I slept as well as I have in years. I'm pretty sure it's the bed." They both chuckled. "I was hoping to wake up and this all be a bad dream. But no such luck." Cassie sighed, sitting up and taking a sip of coffee. Her heart physically hurt. Her eyelids were heavy and swollen. Her cheeks were raw from salty tears.

"Attagirl." Sarah laughed as Cassie crammed in a big bite of bacon to make it all better.

"Have you heard from anyone?" Cassie asked nonchalantly.

"Yes. John, of course. I told you that yesterday. Rick has called, but I haven't returned his messages." She paused. "And I just got off the phone with Liz."

Cassie's chewing stopped and, with her mouth still crammed with food, she somehow managed to get out a word. "And...?"

"I don't want to talk about it yet, and I don't think you're ready to either. It's typical Liz, though. She's sorry, but yet she's the victim. You don't need to hear that right now. Finish up brekky and I'll meet you downstairs. Hal should be home soon." Sarah stroked Cassie's hair, placing one of her golden locks behind her ear.

"Can you believe yesterday we were hundreds of miles apart on the phone talking about Project P.I., pissed that our investigation had come to a roadblock over a burner phone? Little did we know, the case would be solved so quickly, and with *this* ending." Cassie sighed. "We wouldn't have imagined it in a million years."

"No, I definitely didn't see this one coming." Sarah shook her head in disbelief as she left Cassie to her breakfast.

Cassie hesitated to think of who had called her since yesterday. She stared at her phone. She hadn't even looked at it since her call to Sarah on her way to seek refuge. She could only imagine the string of missed voicemails and texts. Picking it up, she had never seen that many notifications appear on her screen before. Twenty-five calls, ten voicemails, and fourteen texts just from Rick. Quickly, she deleted them all.

The rattling of the garage door opening below her bedroom indicated Hal had finally made it home from the hospital. Cassie looked like a close version of death, but somehow managed to get dressed in some clothes that Sarah had lent her, brush her hair and teeth with the stash of guest bathroom commodities available, and look somewhat like a human before heading downstairs to see him, despite what she really felt like—a zombie.

She wasn't sure how much Sarah had let Hal know about her spontaneous visit or the reasoning behind it, but Hal didn't seem a bit shocked to see her come strolling down the stairs, so Sarah must've filled him in on some, if not all, of the dirty details. Hal's outstretched arms beckoned a big hug, to which Cassie obliged. Despite her strongest willpower, she burst into tears.

"What in the world? I am so sorry." It was clear that despite Hal's gentle tone, he was struggling to find the right words to say. She nodded, acknowledging his compassion. "What did you say to them? What did they say?"

"Hal, honey, Cassie may not be ready to talk about it yet," Sarah said to her husband, trying to discretely hint for him to shut up, as she placed a plate of food on the table for him and refreshed Cassie's coffee.

"Oh, it's fine, Sarah. I will have to talk about it at some point," Cassie reassured her overprotective friend, wiping her eyes and somehow pulling herself back together as they both sat down at the table. "Hal, to answer your questions, I couldn't speak. I think they were talking and trying to make excuses, but honestly, the words were a roar in my ears. I wanted to flee as fast as I could."

"Do you know what you're going to do?" Hal asked, while masking a yawn. Hal must have been exhausted from being up all night, but he wasn't about to excuse himself to sleep when his wife's best friend needed to talk. Sarah was so blessed to have found him. He was sweet, cute, smart, and so selfless.

"No, I haven't gotten much past the realization that this wasn't a bad dream." Cassie faked a yawn and excused herself to her room to spare Hal any more of her torturous story and to get some alone time to think and process everything...her new life.

She crept back into the sheets with questions popping up like unwanted weeds in her mind. *How can I go back home? I need clothes and my things. I have to work. Where will I live? I don't think I could ever sleep in that bed again. When will I have the strength to talk to Rick and what would I say?* She wasn't sure if it was all of the fresh uncertainty of her life or the smidge of a hangover from the previous night's bourbon that made a wave of nausea come across her midsection. She closed her eyes and prayed. She prayed for direction. She prayed for solace. And she prayed for all this pain to somehow turn into happiness greater than she could ever imagine on her own. God granted her immediate relief as she drifted off into a peaceful slumber.

CHAPTER THIRTEEN

Liz

DRESSER DRAWERS SLAMMED shut as John rummaged through his clothes, pulling out random pieces and slapping them hard into his luggage. Liz stood by the suitcase, shaking. Never in all of this mess, did she ever picture this part of the story. She had been so reckless, so careless. Not only was she negligent in hiding her love affair, but she had been audacious in boasting about her unhappiness in her marriage to John. Deep down, she wondered if she had *wanted* John to find out. But she had never actually pictured what it would look like once he did. Seeing him there in that moment, in pain and anger, hit her like a ton of bricks. She was overcome with fear—fear of life without John, fear of life without her best friends, and fear of life without Rick. And then there was Paul and Sam. What would she tell them? Sure, they were smart and well-adjusted boys, but the ramifications of a parental split had selfishly never crossed her mind. Shame and embarrassment filled her soul. She wanted to say something to John, something to make it better and fix everything, but she knew nothing could fix this mess she had created. She reached out instead and grabbed John's hand as he was zipping the suitcase closed. He pulled back so firmly and abruptly that it startled her, causing her to jump back as if she had touched a hot stove.

"Don't!" John yelled, breathing heavy and fighting

back tears. "You! You don't get to touch me now. My life, my *entire* life I have devoted to loving you. We have built a home that most people dream of. There is nothing I wouldn't have done, no extreme too outlandish, no request too far-fetched that I wouldn't have done to make you happy. But instead, you threw it all away. Why? I need to know why!" John yelled at the top of his lungs, his face turning red from anger he could not control. Liz shook her head, her eyes begging him to stop.

"I want to know when this started. I want to know how you pulled this off without the two people closest to you finding out. I want to know all of the disgusting, pathetic details."

"John, you don't want to know all of that," Liz begged him.

"Oh, but I do! And now isn't the time for you to tell me what I want and what I don't. What I want is the truth, which I obviously haven't been getting from you lately. I'm hoping that, somewhere in your story, I'll be able to figure out why you would destroy people you love. Now sit! And start talking," John grabbed Liz by her shoulders and forced her down onto the blue and white pinstriped chair next to their bed.

"Last Thanksgiving," Liz whispered, closing her eyes in pain from the memory. "Friendsgiving weekend to be exact. We had dinner here, and you and Hal were cooking steaks on the grill. Cassie and Sarah were finishing up the sides and you realized we were missing rosemary for the steaks. I offered to go grab some and Rick said he would ride with me to the store." Liz sighed from the torture of confession. But John wasn't satisfied.

"And? Keep going," he coaxed, not giving her even a sliver of a break to gather her thoughts.

"We talked. A lot. Well, as much as you can in a ten-minute car ride to Whole Foods. He confessed that Cassie was a mad woman about a baby, and he missed her being intimate with him because she wanted to, not because she had an agenda. I confessed that I was feeling old and washed up, for a lack of better terms. I missed feeling sexy and turning heads. I missed being noticed. Especially by you."

"Me? You're the only woman I have ever even looked twice at. Why in the world would you have ever felt that way?" John was clearly in shock at her words.

"I know but hear me out. Paul and Sam aren't babies anymore. They don't *need* me like they used to. And as far as our patients, they want a female doctor that looks the part, like Kelly. They want someone with flawless skin and a ripped body. I work long hours and have birthed two kids, which doesn't exactly lead to a swimsuit model figure, which is why I decided to do the triathlon. I needed something, someone, to fill the void." Liz looked down at her tanned and muscular hands. They weren't feminine in the least. They were strong and precise with bulging veins and swollen knuckles. How many facelifts and nose jobs and breast implants had they so meticulously performed? Thousands. Those hands had instilled confidence and self-esteem into the lives of so many people over the years, but they couldn't fix the damage to her own self-image. "And then came Kelly. She is beautiful, smart, funny, and everything I used to be. Sure, I should take my experience and reputation and let that fill me up, but I couldn't. I was so threatened. In my mind, I was convinced that you would leave me for her, if not now, then eventually."

"Liz, there is not a chance in this world—" John disputed, but Liz cut him off.

"I said let me finish. You asked me to talk, so let me do it!" she barked with frustration. It had taken every ounce of energy and might she possessed to say those words. If John stopped the momentum, she may not be able to start back up again. "So, when Rick and Cassie left that night, he hugged me bye and told me he was here for me and that we could always confide in each other. He offered to help me train for the triathlon and suggested meeting for drinks that week to come up with a training plan. From that point on, we were talking and texting about everything from our marriages to our daily recaps." She swallowed hard. Her next words would hurt John more than the physical intimacy. "Rick became my confidant, my best friend. I told him things I didn't think I could tell you anymore. I told him my needs and my wants, and he told me his. We wanted the same things, to feel irresistible rather than just needed."

Liz watched cautiously waiting to see his reaction. She was sure the thought of another man making his wife feel a way that he no longer could made him enraged. As she saw his eyes fill with tears for the first time, Liz wondered where they had lost touch? Witnessing his pain, she wanted to stop. This was the most agonizing truth she had ever spoken to him. "Please. That's enough," she begged.

"For now. I need to digest this," he conceded, his eyes looking coldly into hers. "Is he who you want? I need to know. I haven't heard anything so far to make me think what you did was justified. I don't even know if we can be fixed, but I sure as hell won't waste my time trying to if you want him."

Liz stared down at the floor. She wanted it all. She wanted John at her side, her beck and call. But she longed for the excitement and passion and intimacy that Rick gave her. "I don't know," she muttered. "And that is the truth."

Without another word, John grabbed his suitcase and barreled past her. Liz followed desperately as he bolted out of the house, slamming the door behind him hard enough to make the pictures on the walls shake. Liz stood there in silence as she watched her favorite family photo fall from its spot on the wall, glass shattering into a million pieces as it hit the floor. Liz sank to the ground sobbing, staring at the broken pieces of her life.

CHAPTER FOURTEEN

Cassie

THE FLICKERING OF candlelight danced across the walls of the dark bedroom. Flannel sheets warmed by body heat swaddled them together in a tight cocoon. Miles Davis played a low tune from the speakers in the next room. Dishes still sat on the table from the meal he had prepared for her. He was a good cook, but his best talent was pleasure. And he knew just how to satisfy her. He knew how to hold her. No words had to be spoken. Their common language was touch. For two people who loved to talk, being silent ironically seemed much more intimate in each other's presence. Dylan's hand grasped her scalp as he held her hair tightly between his fingers, intentionally pulling just enough to cause her head to tilt back, giving him access to one of his favorite parts of her body. He buried his face into her neck, holding her closely underneath him. She was completely his. And he was completely hers. Her arms wrapped tightly around his neck, hanging on desperately. She knew his soul. She could see straight into it as she stared at his face.

"I love you, Cassie," he whispered into her lips. They were a perfect fit, in every single way. Their hearts beat in sync, their eyes blinked in sync, and their bodies felt pleasure in sync. There was nothing like it in the world, and Cassie was convinced that he was made for her. Her person—or rather, her kryptonite. He was the one man who would always have the biggest piece of her heart and soul. As he curled up behind her, she felt his arm wrap around her as he grabbed her left hand. Stroking her ring finger with his thumb, he whispered in her ear, "I don't ever want to be without you." Cassie smiled at his hint of marriage. He had been a bit gun-shy about taking the next step, so she was gentle in her answer. Any move too abrupt and he might be scared away.

She squeezed his hand acknowledging his words. "Then make me yours."

———◆———

Cassie's eyes opened and she was nearly blinded by the bright sun shining in through the windows of Sarah's guest bedroom. She had to blink a few times in order to make out the person leaning over her. It was John, stroking her hair to awaken Sleeping Beauty. Cassie blushed at the sight of him, hoping that she hadn't let on that she was dreaming of Dylan. How long had John been at her side while she slept?

"Hey, chick. You okay?" He smiled, patting her leg. Typical John, worrying about someone else rather than his own immediate pain.

"I'm still in shock. But more importantly, how are you?" Cassie cupped his tanned face in return, which was always perfectly shaven, even in dire straits. He looked well put together, as a matter of fact, much better than she imagined she must look. The only giveaway of sadness she could detect was his bloodshot eyes indicating he had been crying.

John sighed and looked down at his wedding band. His face turned dark, and she could feel his soul collapse on itself. "I'm defeated," he confessed.

Cassie smiled softly, tears filling her eyes, and gave him an understanding nod.

Sarah and Hal were happy to see Cassie had awoken from the dead as they plopped down on the bed beside her. There they were. Their own real-life *Grey's Anatomy* episode.

"Hey, aren't you guys supposed to be at work or something?" Cassie asked as she scanned her company.

"There's no way I could work today. Not after having a massive Chernobyl bomb dropped on me. I figured the least Liz could do is take care of the boys and hold down the office with Kelly's help," John said shrugging, then looking to Sarah and Hal for their responses.

"Hal has been on call for several days, so he is off today, and I cancelled patients. I'm not leaving you here alone. The four of us spend every day of our lives taking care of others. Right now, we need to take care of us," Sarah reassured Cassie, squeezing her hand. Cassie smiled, knowing that her friend was right. It wasn't every day that your world came crashing down around you. She was so thankful for the safe haven and her precious friendships. But she couldn't help but feel a twinge of sadness. It just seemed so strange without Liz being there, and her heart sank knowing it would never be the same again.

The next hour was spent recounting how the four of them could have missed the signs of Rick and Liz's affair. Sarah and Cassie filled Hal and John in on *Mission: Penis Identification* and Liz's Favorite Mistake. Despite the circumstances, they did manage to have a few laughs out of their covert mission stories. The more they talked, the more everything seemed clearer. John recounted Liz's timeline description of the affair. As painful as it was to hear, the sequence made sense. The distance in their relationship made sense. The reckless behavior from Liz made sense.

"Are you thinking you want to try and work it out?" Sarah asked both John and Cassie.

"I haven't even spoken to Rick. He's blown up my phone wanting to talk, but I can't yet. I don't think I could ever trust him again. It would be different had it been a one-time slip up, but it sounds like they had a true connection, and that's one thing I can't swallow." Cassie sighed as the words trailed out of her mouth. She knew how that connection felt and she also was becoming aware of how those feelings never really went away, proven in point by her subconscious desire for Dylan. Of course, Cassie's opportunity with Dylan had passed, but her connection to him wouldn't. That was something you couldn't shake.

"I don't have a fucking clue what I'm going to do. My whole life has been chasing the coattails of that crazy-ass woman. Our entire world is intertwined. Trying to unravel the mess of work, our kids, and years of memories would be almost impossible. But I honestly don't think Liz knows what she wants either. And if I go back to her, she will never see what it's like to be without me. I think if I stand a chance of piecing us back together, then I have to let her sink on her own. As tough as that may be to watch." John buried his face in his hands in despair.

"You two are more than welcome to stay here as long as you like. You know that," Sarah reassured both of them.

"That is so sweet, Sarah, but this could quickly turn into a bad *Friends* episode if we aren't careful." Cassie smirked.

"What's so wrong with that?" John rebutted sarcastically.

"I think a good round of beers and wings would make us all feel a little better. My treat," Hal suggested, motioning for them to get up and moving.

After three rounds of beers and too many wings to count, Cassie was able to muster up a little more confidence to check the one zillion texts Rick had sent. But nothing could have prepared her for the rage she felt while reading his words. They only made her more upset despite his desperation.

Cassie. Call me. Please. 911.

Cas. I love you. I can't be without you. I made a huge mistake. Please talk to me.

Baby, I will do anything ANYTHING to make this right. It's all my fault.

"Cassie, what are you doing? Are you looking at your texts?" Sarah asked, surprised at Cassie's timing as she watched her friend's face turn red while she held her phone at the restaurant table.

"Yes. I'm drunk. I'm safe with you guys. And I'm in a public place. I'm least likely to lose my shit here in front of other people." Cassie flashed a just-go-with-it look to her friend, signaling her to not press the subject any farther. Sarah obliged.

Cassie continued as she flipped to the screen shot of what they now knew was Rick's penis. "How did I not freaking know it was my husband's dick? Probably because he would be the last person I would ever dream of being my best friend's *Favorite Mistake*," Cassie huffed. "And let's be honest, it's not like penises have any kind of true identifying traits, unless they're extra-large or extra-small, or have a weird piercing, tattoo, or anomaly," Cassie argued, defending her lack of observation to herself and her friends as she took another huge gulp of beer.

"True. A penis is a penis," Sarah added supportively. "What?" she shrugged her shoulders and asked innocently, blowing off her comment as Hal gave her an annoyed look.

"Rick's penis is a typical penis with no special identifying factors, especially when it's cropped, blurry, and the only identifiable object in the image." Or was it? Cassie zoomed in closer on the pattern of underwear in the image. Of course, she hadn't looked this closely before because, well, it was gross and weird to examine a foreign penis. Or it was before now, when it wasn't her own husband's private parts. There, in the corner of the picture, was the edge of a small pirate flag.

"Wait. Look." She handed the zoomed image over to Sarah. Cassie's eyes filled up with so many tears, she could barely confirm what she was seeing. "Those were the boxers I bought Rick for his birthday in January. We had been out in Ybor City for sushi and had decided to walk around and shop the quirky boutiques. The pirate festival was only a week away, so the stores were filled with buccaneer paraphernalia. Rick spotted a pair of boxers with pirate flags and he just had to have them. I offered to give them to him for his birthday on the condition that he would hold me captive while he was wearing them. He agreed and told me I was the best pirate booty ever. We had the best time laughing and role-playing as we made out on the couch that night. But there they are in the picture that he sent my best friend." Cassie shook her head in disbelief. "And that's no laughing matter. I guess the joke is on me."

"And me," John added. "I don't mean to keep you from going through these motions, Cassie, but it's a little uncomfortable talking about a cock that has been frequenting both my wife and my best friend. I'm not sure I'm ready for this in-depth information just yet."

"Oh, John. I am so sorry." Cassie put her phone away in her purse. Her sadness turned to anger as she realized the damage Liz and Rick had done to so many people. It was time to confront Rick. She had to do it for her sake, and for John's. And she needed some clothes. A Rolling Stones t-shirt and underwear wasn't going to cut it for much longer. Thank goodness she could fit into some of Sarah's things. She vowed to leave Sarah's at sunrise and head back to Tampa.

◆

Her stomach churned and gurgled with nervous jitters as her car approached the South Tampa mission-style house. PTSD was setting in from the last time she had pulled into her garage unannounced, unknowingly about to find her husband and best friend all tangled up in her sheets. Instantly, she felt the need to run again. She wanted it all to go away. Rick must have heard the garage door open because he was standing anxiously in the doorway as she pulled in. He looked like shit. Cassie could tell from the bags under his eyes and the gray stubble that had far outgrown its welcome on his face that he hadn't done much sleeping or showering. *I sure hope he has showered since I caught him with Liz,* she thought to herself. The thought of her scent still being on him fueled her anger even more.

"Cassie! Thank God! I…I don't know what to say…" Rick's voice quivered, and his hands shook as he reached out to grab the car door. Once again, Cassie was mute, unable to find any words to say.

As she walked past him in silence into their once bright and homey kitchen, she was slapped in the face with pain. The walls appeared ashy and the air suffocating. The decorations that had once brought her so much joy and comfort from memories of the life they had built together now looked cheap and chintzy. As she faced Rick, still silent, she almost bumped into him. He was right at her heels. Cassie took a long step back slowly with her arms stretched out as if she was backing away from an angry attack dog.

"Away. Stay away," she whispered as her voice shook. Rick's eyes filled with pain as he slumped back in rejection. "It's yours. All of it. I don't want a single thing. Not a single memory. It's all a lie."

"Cassie, please. Just let me explain. I can explain. It's all my fault," Rick pleaded, his hands running nervously through his hair. As he tried to grab her in an effort to pull her in close to him, she pushed her hands into his chest, hard. All she could think about was Liz laying on the firm body she used to find such comfort in.

"No. Do. Not. Touch. Me." she said with venom in her voice as she headed into the bedroom. Cassie felt faint as she walked back toward the crime scene. She had to get her things and get out of there as quickly as possible.

"But I love you. You're my wife. I made an awful, horrible mistake in a time of weakness and I will do anything, and I mean *anything*, to fix this. I want to be with you, be the father of your children, grow old with you," Rick begged as he followed her every move. Cassie stopped suddenly in her tracks as Rick's words struck a chord inside her. With an armful of scooped up clothes and hangers from the closet, she spun around like poltergeist on steroids.

"How *dare* you say that to me! You know all I ever wanted was those things. But *you* ruined it. *You*, Rick, destroyed *our* dreams. Maybe you should have thought about repercussions prior to sending pictures of your dick to my best friend and fucking her behind my back." And with that, she stormed past him and out the door, leaving him in a trail of disgust.

CHAPTER FIFTEEN

Rick

RICK STARED AT his computer screen. He had three documents due by the end of the day that couldn't be postponed, or he would be out of a job. But there was only one thing on his mind. Cassie. How could he have ever been so foolish? Cassie was his wife, his lover, and his friend. Yes, she had turned into somewhat of a controlling baby-making monster, but that was one of the reasons he had fallen in love with her: her determination. He loved the fact that she never settled and never took no for an answer. She set her goals and conquered each one, some with ease and some with tenacity, but always in comple tion. But the fun of their marriage had been withering away. He felt like he was being used for an agenda, and he was exhausted. He was tired of her emotional roller-coasters. Sure, she was on tons of hormones that didn't help the situation, but it was like walking on eggshells. She controlled everything from his travel schedule to his underwear size. Part of him wanted to rebel, to sabotage her plans. Maybe he wanted to know that if their future didn't hold children, he alone would be enough to make her happy.

He picked up the phone one more time, hoping that this time, she might answer. Seeing her so hurt and angry with him gnawed at his soul. He had never seen her like that before. He dialed her number and heard her voice for what seemed like the hundredth time on her voicemail. His heart ached even more hearing the sound of it.

The ping of a text interrupted the end of her words just as Cassie's voicemail tone beeped and he hung up.

Please call me. We have to talk. We need to talk.

It was Liz. Rick would have to face her at some point, but right now, he couldn't focus on anything but his wife.

Not now, he responded. He wanted Liz to know where he stood. He wanted her to know that they had to end. They couldn't *be.*

Please, Rick. I know you're hurting too. We can fix this.

Liz's words incited a wave of anger that he could not control. He dialed Liz with his heart racing and his face beet red. He heard her pick up.

"How in the hell do you think we can fix this? Haven't we done enough damage already? If you think us being together or working as a team to try and clear up this mess will help everyone heal, then you're delusional. Liz, I was attracted to you because of your zest, your free spirit attitude that Cassie never possessed. But I have come to see that all of that is a façade. Under your armor, you're a weak and needy woman looking for anything to make you feel special, and that, Liz, is *your* problem, not mine. I want to talk to my *wife.* And I suggest that you try to contact that same person who happens to be one of your *best friends* who did *nothing* to deserve what we did to her!" And with that, he hung up and slammed his phone down on his desk and swatted a pile of papers, causing them to swirl around in the air before they landed like confetti on the floor of his office.

CHAPTER SIXTEEN

Liz

LIZ SAT THERE still holding her phone to her ear despite the crippling silence coming from the other end. Rick was right. He was so very right about everything. Why would the one person she craved to talk to be *him* when she had a marriage and a friendship racing dangerously toward a crashing waterfall—or maybe they had already plummeted to their death. Maybe that's why she was numb. Maybe it was just too late. The damage had been done. Months ago, she had mourned the loss of her best friend. Of course, Cassie didn't know then that their trust had been broken, but Liz had. She had tried so hard to be normal around Cassie, but she just couldn't, overwhelmed with guilt and jealously. Part of her had felt terrible that she was fucking her best friend's husband and the other part of her had felt overcome with resentment that Cassie got to wake up next to Rick every day.

It was barely five o'clock, but Liz headed to the wine cooler anyway. She grabbed a crisp French rosé and a wine goblet and headed to her sunroom, hoping to find some sort of peace or maybe even some answers to her messy life. As she hopelessly sunk into her white wicker chair, she lifted her feet to rest on the burlwood coffee table. Her eyes caught a glimpse of the photo album placed haphazardly in the seagrass basket underneath the table. The blue leather album had been there for years, holding images of memories that had made everyone in them smile, until now.

Liz reached down with shaking hands to grab the precious piece of history. As she flipped open the cover, her heart sank even further into her chest. There they were, the five med students that were inseparable. She and John were all tangled up in a smoochy hug as usual, with smiles that were so truthful and real. Dylan had his arms around Sarah and Cassie, his hand grabbing Cassie's butt cheek, so she was caught mid scream in the photo. It had been one of their favorite memories to recount. A smile crept across her face as she remembered that night, filled with way too many shots, way too much dancing in high heels, and walking home with no shoes on. Of course, the shots had numbed her dainty feet, so they'd felt no pain that night. But the next day had told the true tale. Her feet had been raw from the concrete trek and her calves aching from high heels and dancing, so much that she had made John pour hot water and Epsom salts into a Rubbermaid storage tub for her to soak her feet in. She chuckled at the memory of sitting in her pinstriped chair, the one that was now by their bed, in her white plush robe, eating a greasy cheeseburger John had fetched for her and praying for the pain in her feet to stop. She even remembered once asking him to amputate them, and him laughing at her dramatic antics. Why had he done it? Why had John always come to her rescue? No matter the audacity or the ridiculousness of the requests, he had obliged.

As she turned the plastic page over, the crackling sound of pages sticking together produced a gem. Cassie was holding Paul, Liz's oldest son, the day he was born. In that photo, a proud "aunt" with bright, young skin and long, curly blond hair held her first godson. The fair-skinned baby with blond hair like his daddy had grown into a kid that still adored his Aunt Cassie, even when he thought his mom and dad were too lame to even be acknowledged.

As Liz's eyes gazed at the adjacent image, her heart began to pound intensely. Her heart ached and the irony of it all seemed so surreal. Cassie stood eloquently in her wedding gown. She was stunning. As a tall, thin, fit, and sexy doctor, her badass persona had attracted some of the most gorgeous, successful men Liz had ever met. She had been a little jealous of Cassie's ability to get the men most had only dreamed of. From athletes to CEOs, she had gone through what seemed like a hundred men after she and Dylan had parted ways. Liz had imagined that Cassie was still in love with Dylan and that's why she took so long to settle down with someone and commit. And then came Rick. He was different than the rest. He had a swagger and confidence that even Cassie couldn't resist. Liz and Sarah had been suspicious of him and his fidelity from the beginning. He had seemed like he still had a dash of player left. Of course, he had given them no reason to doubt his love and intentions for Cassie. But as Liz stared at the photo, it was eerily prophetic. Cassie was dancing and laughing with John while Rick held Liz, the matron of honor, closely in a slow dance. They were innocent then. Their relationships were easy and fun. There were no complications, no tangled lines crossed. Liz took a long drink of her rosé and then let out a long sigh of defeat. She would never be able to untangle the mess she had made. Not in a million years.

CHAPTER SEVENTEEN

Cassie

THERE WERE PERKS to being a well-known ENT in town. Cassie had a list of high-profile clients a mile long, one of whom happened to be a multimillionaire developer with access to the nicest real estate in South Tampa. He was able to immediately set her up with a furnished long-term rental in a high rise with views of the Tampa Bay that would make anyone jealous. The space, with its modern furniture and sleek finishes, was totally different from the bright white, organic mission-style home she was used to, but that's exactly what she needed. Something totally different.

Her morning coffee was divine on the balcony in the mornings. And wine in the evenings paired with perfect sunsets helped to ease the pain of her new life. The balcony wrapped around the corner of the unit, giving a full panoramic view of blue skies with streaks of orange and pink. The wind blew through the palm fronds, making them dance in perfect rhythm with the waves rolling into the bay. Runners and skaters looked like speckled dots moving along the sidewalk of Bayshore Drive from ten stories up.

Cassie had dreamed of having that view. She had pleaded with Rick on multiple occasions for them to buy a house along the famous Drive, but he thought it was too pricey and too busy for a growing family. After all, he argued, they would have added expenses of private school, nannies, and all the other millions of things that kids required. Cassie snickered as she stared out over the balcony. Ironically, she got this view in the end anyway. Just not in the way she had planned.

The hospital had been eerily quiet over the past few weeks since the affair had been uncovered. Cassie was certain that Liz had been avoiding the concrete walls as much as possible, too, hoping not to cross paths with her. She still hadn't spoken to Liz. Multiple times she had pondered what she might say once she had the courage and energy to confront her, but no words seemed to accurately describe how hurt she was. But it was inevitable that she would see Liz and be forced to either speak or ignore her. It was going to be a game time decision as to how she would react.

John seemed to be functioning as best as possible. He had rented a short-term condo since he and Liz were still barely on speaking terms. Paul and Sam had been bouncing back and forth between parents but seemed to be handling the situation well despite the circumstances. Furthermore, Cassie could only imagine the awkwardness that Liz and John had been experiencing in their practice on a day-to-day basis. Their lives were so intermingled. There was no way for them to truly separate from each other. John's aim was to force Liz to realize what life would be like without him, but Cassie just didn't see where Liz would ever get that opportunity. And then there was Kelly. Surely being in the middle of that mess wasn't what she had signed up for when she took the associate position.

As fate would have it, as Cassie rounded the corner coming out of the ER, she almost ran smack dab into Liz.

"Shit!" Liz stopped abruptly to avoid spilling her coffee on her white coat, not noticing who her face-off was against. An awkward silence struck both of them as their eyes met. Cassie's heartbeat imploded in her chest and fight-or-flight instincts kicked into full gear.

"Oh. Um. Hey, Cassie. I'm sorry. I didn't see you coming," Liz awkwardly squeaked out. Her eyes had left Cassie's stare and landed sheepishly on the ground, but Cassie's intense gaze never wavered. Cassie's quick tongue found it hard to control itself.

"That makes the second time in a row you didn't expect my appearance, huh, Liz?" The words were mean, and she didn't care. While she couldn't physically harm Liz, she could hurt her with her lashing words, and it felt good.

"I deserve that." Liz swallowed hard, still looking down at her white snakeskin heels. "I know this isn't the best place to talk, but I have wanted to call you so many times. But Sarah—"

"Sarah said all you need to know, Liz," Cassie stated, cutting her off from any bullshit excuse. "I don't need your apologies or lame ass excuses about why you felt it was justifiable for you to fuck my husband. As far as I'm concerned, you can have your *Favorite Mistake* with a side of *fuck you* and live happily ever after." As Cassie stepped past Liz to exit fight mode and enter flight, Liz grabbed her arm.

"How did you and Sarah get into my phone? Rick told me you did it in Charleston when I was passed out." Liz's suspicious stare pierced Cassie with curiosity.

"Does it really matter at this point? We all have our secrets, now, don't we?" And with that, Cassie pulled her arm away. She couldn't get to her car fast enough.

Cassie sat there, staring out of her windshield, hands clasped hard on the steering wheel, part of her regretting not being more aggressive and part of her proud at her quick wit. She dialed Sarah. She needed to hear her voice. She needed her comfort and security.

"Hey, chick. Break away from the hospital?" Sarah answered cheerfully.

"Not fast enough, unfortunately." Cassie's disappointed tone let Sarah know that something had happened.

"Oh, no. You ran into Liz, didn't you?"

"Yes." She let out a deep breath. "We almost crashed right into each other. I didn't have time to escape or hide, and she didn't either."

"Well, that's probably a good thing. I can imagine that you can now breathe a sigh of relief having gotten the confrontation over with. You can't spend your life running from her. It's been weeks now and you haven't so much as tried to contact her. I don't blame you, but you won't heal until you feel vindicated in some way."

"I can't imagine healing at all right now. All I can do is focus on putting one foot in front of the other in a series of motions to get through my days. It's the first time in my life when I don't have my future planned out by the minute. My life has been filled with goals, agendas, and dreams. My prayer each day now is to simply make it through seeing my patients without tapping out mentally in the middle of a procedure. I've even contemplated taking a sabbatical from my practice to try and pull my shit together, but honestly, I think it's the only thing keeping me from unraveling."

"I agree. Working and seeing patients is tough when you're hurting, but you need to still do it in order to keep yourself sane. It gives you a sense of accomplishment. I was actually going to call you tonight anyway and ask if you had heard from any of your partners about the ENT continuing education course that's here in Savannah in a few weeks. It would be a great tax deductible reason for you to come visit Hal and me. You could stay here if you wanted, and we could meet you downtown for drinks and dinner when your classes are over. Please, please, please! What else do you have to do but sit in that gorgeous condo?" Sarah's begging would have rivaled any of her pediatric patients.

"I remember getting an email about it a few weeks ago, but honestly, I've been in such a daze that it didn't register. I can't imagine sitting in class all day right now, trying to focus on nasopharyngeal surgery and sinusitis. Can I think about it? I guess I do still have some CE hours that I need before the end of the year."

"Great! Hal will be so excited. Come on down Thursday after work and your bed will be waiting. Love you, sister."

"Love you, more." Cassie wasn't sure if she was up for it, but it sure would be nice to have something to look forward to. "Who knows, maybe I'll learn something life changing. I will check my schedule and see if I am on call that weekend. Keep you posted." And she hung up, thankful for her pushy friend who always knew what she needed even before she did.

———◆———

Cassie couldn't remember the last night of good sleep she had gotten in weeks. Most of her nights had been filled with restless tossing and turning until she finally lightly dozed off, only to be awakened by her wretched alarm at five fifteen. It was all she could do to make it to the espresso machine, craft a double shot, and pile on layers of eye cream to start the day. The amount of caffeine she consumed each day was enough to jumpstart any dead battery. Her hands shook from the amps, and the fact that food was the last thing on her mind didn't help the situation. She was dropping weight each week without even trying. Her bras were beginning to gape from her withering boob mass, and her pants were sagging from her disappearing backside. She had previously packed on a little weight with all the fertility hormones, but since she hadn't taken any of those in a couple months now, she had dropped way below her average weight. She had been relying on her hospital scrubs and their drawstring

waistbands for work. Social outings had been non-exis-
tent, so it hadn't been an issue that most of the clothes
in her closet looked like a garbage bag hanging on her
slender body. Somehow, she had managed to find some
clothes to pack for the continuing education course in
Savannah that Sarah had talked her into attending. She
had waited until the last minute to register for it, so she
hadn't had time to shop for anything to take. Thankfully,
her black wrap top was perfect. It was adjustable to her
new waist size, and low cut enough to make her feel
sexy, but still professional. Cassie never went anywhere
without her black high heels. They were the epitome of
business sleek and comfortable as hell. She could have
run a marathon in them. She took one last look in her
rearview mirror to check her lip gloss before heading
toward the large double doors of the Savannah Westin
Hotel and Convention Center.

The view upon entering the hotel was stunning. The
glass wall of windows framed the picturesque Savannah
River Street and waterway. The old buildings were gorgeous with their gray brick and mortar. The canopy of
live oaks and Spanish moss blew around happily in the
breeze coming off the water. A massive barge the size of
an entire block somehow floated down the river toward
the ports. Cassie smiled. She had made the right decision
to visit for the weekend. She could feel her stress level
and her heart rate lower. This city had magical powers
for her. Even during medical school, the five of them
would sneak off some weekends to a cheap hotel room
on Tybee Island just to get away from the hustle and bustle of Atlanta. They would walk the streets of downtown
Savannah until the wee hours of the morning, drinks
in hand, stumbling around on the cobblestone pathways.
They would cram their hungover bellies with grease
from The Breakfast Club, then bake for hours in the sand
near the pier. It was their fun little escape. It's also when

Sarah had fallen in love with the city. When she'd gotten a job offer at Memorial Hospital's pediatric unit, she'd known it was meant to be. Cassie and Liz hadn't fought her on the decision to move to Savannah rather than Tampa. They knew why she loved it because they loved it too.

The chilly conference room was filled with men and women alike. All were smart. Some were old, some young, some were attractive, and some were opportunists. They were the prime examples of high school nerds that had taken full advantage of recreating themselves on social media. Liz liked to refer to them as "doctor hot." As an average Joe, no one would take a second look at them. But give them a stethoscope and *bam*, they had the Stepford wife and the cookie cutter Pinterest family. Their wives had impressive boob jobs, and their cars smelled of clean leather. They were the guys that in high school that had dreamed of dating the homecoming queen, only to be overlooked in favor of the football star. But in that moment, Cassie didn't care about analyzing any of them. She wanted to find a spot near the back of the cold classroom that she could sit that would allow easy access to escape. Frequent bathroom and coffee breaks would be the key to her survival.

Cassie managed to make it through until the final session of the day. She had already embarrassed herself a few times by nodding off, head bob and all. Sarah had texted that she and Hal wouldn't be wrapping up their day until around six, so Cassie decided to head to the riverfront tiki bar for a glass of wine. The day was gorgeous. The breeze coming off the water was strong enough to keep the no-seeums away, but still way warmer than the overly air-conditioned space she had just spent her day in.

Something felt surreal in that moment as a cold chill ran down her spine. Taking a sip of the crisp, fruity wine, Cassie felt a sense of excitement. Maybe it was the city or the wine, but she was suddenly overcome with a wave of exhilaration for the future. It was something she hadn't felt in years, like an electric charge running through her soul. It was an emotion she could only explain with verbs like *soar* or *leap*. She closed her eyes and smiled. And for the first time in months, she actually felt good. Happy. It was all going to be okay.

And then it all made sense.

A familiar voice behind her made her heart stop as she heard a whisper in her ear and felt a gentle hand touch her lower back. "I sure have missed that smile." In her whole entire life, she could never—would never—forget that voice.

Dylan.

As she turned to make certain this wasn't one of her vivid, life-like dreams of him, her eyes locked on his. In pure instinct, her hand cupped his face and pulled him in close, her arms reaching around his shoulders. And just like that, they fit together once again like a lock and key.

"Oh, my gosh! Dylan! I can't believe it's really you. How have we not run into each other all of these years?" Cassie squealed, waving him to sit down at the high-top table with her.

"I know. It's hard to believe we haven't. I must be completely honest, though: I usually check the course roster for your name. More so just so I can mentally prepare myself for seeing you. But your name has never been listed. Not even for this one."

"Yeah, this one was kind of last minute," Cassie chuckled, taking a sip of wine in an effort to calm her nerves in his presence. She wasn't about to get into all the details with him just yet. Besides, they had years to catch up on. "Sarah made me sign up. She lives here now with her husband, Hal. I registered last minute so I didn't even have a name tag printed out at the registration table for my lanyard."

"That's not like the type A, OCD planner Cassie that I know. Becoming a slacker in your old age, eh?" he smirked as he motioned for the bartender. "Woodford and Coke please, and another glass of wine for the lady."

"There's a lot that's different about me now." Cassie smiled back at him, implying a few hidden secrets.

"Oh, really now? I can't wait to hear. Are you here alone?" She saw Dylan's eyes gaze across her left hand. The rings were gone, but the indentation and white tan line hadn't yet faded.

"Um, yes. I'm staying with Sarah and Hal. He is a pediatric cardiologist, so they're both still at the hospital. I'm just here killing time before dinner with them." Cassie fiddled with the base of her wine glass nervously. She hadn't been around a man she had chemistry with besides her husband in years. It was weird. She was sure Dylan noticed the fidgeting as she saw him eyeing her fingers and smiling, obviously still proficient in reading her body signs, no matter how much Cassie claimed to have evolved.

"As much as I would like to see Sarah, I really would love to catch up on you first. Something tells me we have a lot to talk about." He reached out to her fidgeting left hand and grabbed it, squeezing it tightly. Cassie tried hard, but she couldn't hide her excitement from his touch.

"That sounds wonderful. Let me go call Sarah. I'm sure she will take a raincheck. Especially if she knows it's for you. If you will excuse me." Cassie somehow pulled away from Dylan's tight grip and his stare to make her way to the hotel lobby. She was shaking so intensely she could barely dial Sarah's number.

"Hey. Hal and I are just about to head home and shower. Where do ya wanna go? The Olde Pink House? I know it's your fave," Sarah answered.

"Um, actually that's what I'm calling about. You might

want to sit down for this one. It's Dylan. He's here. With me. Having a drink."

"What the fuck?! Holy shit! Um, *okay*. So, are you okay? Did you faint? Oh, my gosh, I need details!"

"I know. I'm just as shocked as you are. After all these years and I run into him now? Here? He wants to go to dinner with me. Is it okay if I take a raincheck?"

"Totally. But only if I get every single minute detail when you get in tonight. Deal?"

"Deal." She hung up and walked past a wall mirror hanging in the lobby, checking out her makeup and hair. *Ugh. I totally would have worn something more fitting for a reunion with my ex-boyfriend. And I most definitely would have freshened up my makeup,* Cassie thought as she straightened her black wrap top and fluffed her long, blonde curly hair, marching as confidently as she could back toward the tall, handsome gentleman waiting for her return.

"She said to tell you hello," Cassie fibbed just a little bit, refraining from telling Dylan exactly what their conversation had entailed. She figured he could guess what was really said anyway.

"Aw. I really do want to see her while I'm here. I had no clue she had moved to Savannah. You would think with me being down the road on St. Simon's Island, that her name would have come up. I never bought into the social media world, so I do feel left out at times. I keep up with a few old classmates of ours through email, but I never really heard where Sarah wound up." Dylan reached for his bourbon. Cassie smiled. It was still his drink of choice.

"St. Simon's? I thought you had stayed in Atlanta all these years?" Despite his efforts at staying off the grid, Cassie had managed to keep up with him through internet stalking and random bits of knowledge she had gathered through mutual contacts. But obviously not the ones he kept up with since no one had informed her of his move away from Atlanta.

"Yeah, I got tired of the hustle and bustle. My stress level was rising just as fast as the love for my career was declining. I had nothing keeping me there in the city, so when a job opened up there in Brunswick, I took it. Of course, it's not as glamorous as Emory Hospital, but evening walks on the beach and weekends spent on my fishing boat are way more my style anyway."

"You always did love a boat," Cassie smiled, thinking of all the fun they'd had during the summers on his boat.

"From what I recall, you loved a boat too," he chuckled as he took the last sip of his drink. Cassie blushed immediately, knowing exactly what sexual ventures he was referring to. Their boat sexcapades had long been a common theme in her recurring dreams. There was just something primal about being all alone, for as far as the eye could see, and making love in the wide-open daylight.

"I won't argue that." Cassie tried to stay cool but was pretty sure her pink cheeks gave away the imagery in her mind. "Obviously, those trips left quite an impression on you as well."

"I won't argue that," he rebutted cheekily. "Speaking of boats, let's go catch the ferry across the river. We can walk around downtown and find a good dinner spot. Any ideas?" Dylan motioned for the check and Cassie quickly caught a glimpse of his left hand. No ring, no indentation, no tan line. She had to make sure there wasn't anything else she had missed from the poor-quality sources of Dylan intel.

As they made their way onto the ferry, the wind from the water blew past Dylan and onto her skin, a welcomed cooling breeze through her hair. It also caught the scent of Dylan's cologne and, just like any familiar scent, she was taken back years into her past. It was masculine and warm. It took all the composure she had not to bury her face in the nape of his neck. Nothing in the world smelled as good as someone you love. And they had loved. A lot.

It had been so many years, but the familiarity of his hand on her lower back as he guided her onto the ferry, and the firm and gentlemanly grip he had on her hand as she stepped up onto the deck of the boat, were not awkward or unsettling at all. As a matter of fact, it felt eerily natural, like no time had passed at all. Dylan's mannerly gestures were innate to him. Growing up in South Georgia, he was the only son of a debutante mother who had prided herself in raising the perfect Southern gentleman. He had grown up on a farm, so hard work and discipline had been ingrained in him from an exceedingly early age, as well as his marksmanship skills. He was a sharp-shooter with an extreme talent for hunting and fishing. Cassie had teased him that his excellent surgical hand skills had come from all the deer he had field dressed and fish he had cleaned. To her, there was something so sexy about his "hunter/gatherer" persona that made her feel safe and extremely feminine.

Her mind flashed back to the one time he had talked her into going deer hunting early one chilly fall morning. She hadn't been too excited about it, but she'd known he really wanted to take her, so she'd gone, camouflage Carhartts and all.

"Do you remember the time you took me deer hunting?" She watched Dylan roll his eyes as the memory popped back into his mind. "You and your dad had spent months fabricating that Taj-Mahal of a deer stand, which to me looked like a big boy version of a tree house."

"Yes. I remember. I also remember how terrible of a hunting partner you were. You were very distracting." Dylan smiled.

"I agree. I definitely didn't want to go. But once I was up there, I finally understood what you meant by the peacefulness of being in nature. There were no sounds of cars, no cell phones ringing, and no televisions. Just birds chirping and frogs croaking and the wind rustling through the fall-colored leaves. I will never forget it. It was magical." And so was he. Despite his laser like focus on the field that lay ahead of them, Cassie had been able to break his mission for a few minutes with a simple hand across his thigh and kiss on his neck. After all, they were in the middle of nature. Why not let nature take its course?

"You were so annoyed with me by the end of the trip." Cassie laughed, remembering how angry he'd gotten that he'd missed a buck because of their sex break, even though he'd tried his best to hide his agitation.

"And I guess you noticed you never got invited again."

"Oh, for that I was thankful. I had seen and done all that I wanted to from the one tour I had experienced. I was fine sleeping in a warm bed while I waited for my modern-day Davy Crockett to return with game in tow." Cassie winked at him.

Small talk about work filled the time left on the quick ferry ride. But there were bound to be tough questions ahead at dinner. She hadn't talked about what had happened with Rick to anyone outside her safe circle of friends and her parents. She had been very vague with coworkers and acquaintances about the details of their separation. The thought of coming clean about the whole story made her stomach churn.

They decided on the basement tavern of The Olde Pink House. Cassie's ankles quivered as they tried to stabilize themselves in heels on the old cobblestone sidewalks. As she held tight to Dylan's arm for support, she saw him try to hide a smile as his hand grasped their interlocked arms.

The tavern was Cassie's favorite place to eat in Savannah. Not only was the food amazing, but the venue screamed early American history with its brick walls and solid dark wood casings. There were two wood burning fireplaces surrounded by antique sofas with worn velvet fabrics and well broken-in down cushions placed solely for cocktail conversations that were meant to be remembered. A pianist at the small baby grand piano tucked in the corner played "Moon River," while the sweetest voice accompanied the masterfully executed tune. The talented little old lady had been present every time Cassie had dined there, dressed in debutante cocktail attire and bedazzling jewels. It was one of the things that made this spot so special to Cassie. She hoped Sarah and Hal wouldn't be upset that she had gone ahead to their planned dinner venue without them. As they took a seat at a table in a corner of the quaint space, Cassie's eyes were fixed on how handsome Dylan was. The candlelit table cast a warm glow across his high cheekbones and highlighted the now salt and pepper hair above his ears. Time had served him well in the looks department.

"So, tell me what I should order? I figure you have some menu favorites?" Dylan asked, scanning the menu.

"I love the scored flounder and the fried green tomatoes. Nothing says Southern cuisine like mouthwatering fried vegetables, right?" Cassie chuckled, remembering how much he used to love a good Southern home-cooked meal. She wasn't so fond of that type of food, but he always had been. He would eat at some greasy spoon while she scanned the menu for something that would fit into her diet of salad and grilled chicken.

"Oh, so you're coaching me on fried Southern cuisine now. Time must have expanded your palate to the finer things in life." As they both laughed, Dylan reached across the table and grabbed her hand. His laughter turned to silence as he stared compassionately into her eyes.

"Cassie, I have no idea what happened to you and your marriage. It's not my place to ask. But I know you—or at least at one time knew you—very well. I can tell you've been through something tough and I am so sorry."

She swallowed hard, not sure what exactly would come out of her mouth. All she could muster up was an acknowledging nod. She couldn't say the words just yet. Thankfully, she was saved by the server approaching the table to take their order. But as soon as the server stepped away, Cassie felt a surge of confidence that came from somewhere out of the blue.

"Liz." That was all she could get out before she paused.

"Yeah, how is she? I meant to ask you earlier how she was. Doesn't she live in Tampa too?" Dylan asked innocently. But Cassie's awkward pause continued. "Cassie? Are you okay?" he pried, noticing the tense expression on Cassie's face.

"Yes. Sure. No. Not really." She shook her head in frustration, praying for the courage to speak clearly. "Um, Liz and my husband, Rick, had an affair. I caught them in our bed. It had been going on for months. I haven't really been able to talk about it to anyone but Sarah and John. It just came out a few months ago." She fought back tears and swallowed hard to dislodge the lump in her throat. As difficult as those words were to say, it felt good to hear herself speak them. She was so thankful for Dylan in that moment. This meeting wasn't just chance. God had brought him to her to help her heal somehow.

"What? That's unbelievable. I...I...I am so, so sorry. Why in the world would two people who love you hurt you like that? I just can't imagine what you've been through." Cassie could tell he was searching for the right words to say. "I can promise you that whatever caused that situation to evolve between the two of them had nothing to do with you. They are the broken ones." Dylan's eyes were sincere and kind. He was right. Deep down she had desperately yearned to believe that while she was guilty of weighing down her marriage with a heavy fertility plan, no one deserved what had unfolded. Hearing from an outsider that what had happened wasn't her fault lifted a burden of liability she hadn't been able shake. Overwhelmed with confidence, she rehashed the whole story to Dylan with all of the disgusting details. Maybe it was the wine or the company, but her safety in the moment compelled her to take advantage of her newfound courage.

As they climbed out of the cab at the hotel, Cassie handed her valet tag to the attendant. She hoped Sarah wasn't waiting up for her after her long day at the hospital. She had probably had one too many glasses of wine to drive, but the conversation over dinner was sobering. Before she could say anything, Dylan waved off the valet attendant and put his arm around her waist.

"No need to do that, sir. This gorgeous lady has had way too much to drink to be driving home. I will ensure she gets home safely." Cassie's stomach filled with butterflies as he grabbed her hand, leading her through the automatic doors to the lobby elevator. She didn't resist him at all as he pulled her into the elevator and pushed the number to his floor. Before the doors had barely closed, they were an entangled mess, with their bodies coiled up like a vine. Heavy breathing drowned out the random elevator music as his hands navigated up the back of her shirt like a pro. The doors opened to his floor and with determination he pulled her out of the elevator and down the hall to his room. Once they reached the door, he spun her towards him and grabbed her face with both hands, staring hard into her eyes.

"Are you okay with this?" he questioned sincerely.

Cassie looked confidently into his soul, giving him a coy smile.

"I am wholeheartedly sure." She snatched the key from his hand and opened the door. She wanted him, all of him. Every. Single. Inch. Breezing past him and into the room, she saw him smile as he closed the door behind them with conviction. Cassie kicked off her favorite black heels and crawled on her knees onto the edge of the bed facing him, peeling off the black wrap shirt and tossing it at his feet. He silently stood beside the bed staring at her body in awe.

"Well, are you just going to stand there?" Cassie teased, running her fingers over the collar of his shirt.

"No. I'm just taking in the view. I've missed it. You are so beautiful. You always have been," Dylan whispered leaning in to kiss her breasts as his hands worked furiously to finish removing what was left of her clothes. She unbuttoned his dress shirt as fast as she could, kissing him and pulling him close to her. As she unbuckled his belt and dropped his pants to the floor, he crawled on top of her, engulfing her in his arms. The weight of his body on top of hers made her feel so safe, so protected. One more second was too long to wait. Taking hold of him, she kissed his lips forcing him deep inside of her. They both moaned at the sensation. So perfect. While they moved together in familiar sync, Cassie was overcome with emotion. For the first time in a long time, she felt whole, complete. Just like she had in her dreams of him.

Dylan grasped her hips, rolling onto his back. Pushing Cassie upright, filling her up completely, her soul beamed at finally finding its match. She hadn't loved anyone else like this before. And she knew he hadn't either. As she leaned down to kiss him, their eyes locked on each other, both acknowledging familiar cues. Some things never change. Simultaneously, they squeezed hard into each other, overcome with intense pleasure as Cassie felt his warmth flow inside of her. There wasn't anything more magical or profound: love in its truest form.

After the heavy breathing stopped, Dylan stroked her face, sinking his tongue deep into her mouth. "I have missed you every day. I never want to be without you ever again," he whispered as they both drifted off into the most peaceful sleep, wrapped in each other's arms.

As the sun started to peek through the edge of the drawn curtains, Cassie knew she would have some explaining to do to Sarah. She reached to the bedside table slowly so as not to wake Dylan. He was obviously still a deep sleeper. She couldn't help but giggle at how they had slept. It was just like old times, like they had never missed a beat, with him spooned up behind her, one of his long legs sandwiched in between hers, and his long, muscular arm wrapped around her waist, guarding her from escape. Cassie quickly snapped a picture of their feet tangled up just outside the sheets and sent it to Sarah. The dots of her reply formed before Cassie even thought she could have had time to open the message.

Oh hell! I knew it! Hal owes me a massage.

Seriously? You're placing bets with your husband on my sex life? I will be back in a few to shower.

"Whatcha doing?" Dylan finally woke up and started kissing her neck as she finished texting Sarah. She felt him move his hand in between her legs and her heart rate instantly skyrocketed.

"I wanted Sarah to know I was alive. I feel terrible for not letting her know I was staying with you last night." She rolled over to kiss him.

"She knows us. She used to have to put up with our all-night rendezvousing for years, so I doubt she even expected you to come home," he snickered, kissing her back.

"So, am I *that* easy?" Cassie taunted, playfully slapping him on his shoulder.

"Hey, lady, don't start what you can't finish." He laughed as he jumped on top of her pinning her down with her arms above her head. She could feel him hard between her thighs as he kissed her.

"Dylan, I have got to go shower. As much as I would love to stay for round two, we *do* have class at eight. I doubt any attendees would notice, but as a grown woman, I can't do the walk of shame at a medical convention. I think having the same clothes on from yesterday might be a little too obvious."

"Oh, come on, Cas, you know we'll be quick," he tried convincing her otherwise as his lips tickled her abdomen.

"No, sir," she said, managing to get out from under his grasp somehow.

"Damn. You still have ninja moves. Raincheck? Lunch time maybe?"

"I think that's a good possibility," she agreed, gathering up her clothes from all corners of the room. Cassie leaned in, kissed him, and gave his erection a nice squeeze. "See ya later, big fella." They both snickered. He pulled her in for one last kiss, giving her ass a big slap.

"I'll save you a seat. Don't be late," she heard him yell as she closed the door to his room. There was nothing that could have wiped the smile from her face.

Sarah greeted her at the door with an investigative look and a cup of coffee. "I need details. Now!"

"Okay, but I'm in a hurry, so you're going to have to sit in the bathroom while I get ready. I'm running late." Cassie grabbed the coffee out of Sarah's hand, took a sip, and breezed past her to the shower. Sarah plopped down on the tile floor as steam started to fill the room.

"So? What happened? Well, I *know* what happened. But you know what I mean. Was it the same, better, weird? I need to know!" Sarah belted over the noise of the shower.

"Yes, he still has a big dick. Yes, we still have amazing, toe-curling, dream-about-years-later sex. Are we getting married? I don't know. It felt amazing being back in his arms, and I didn't realize how much I had forgotten what true love felt like. You know, true connection." Cassie swung open the shower curtain to see Sarah curled up in a ball, wrapped in a robe, drinking the coffee Cassie had swiped from her moments ago.

"Hum. Okay. Did you tell him about Liz? He knows you're officially still married, right?"

"Yes and yes," Cassie answered as she twisted her wet hair into a towel.

"So, what's his story? Did he ever marry?"

"No. He had a few serious relationships, but never met the right one."

"Because the right one was you, duh." Sarah rolled her eyes at what seemed to be an obvious observation.

"I don't know. Honestly, we talked a lot about me. Probably too much. For the first time, I actually opened up to someone about what happened, other than you. I felt safe and it was so nice to let it all out. He probably thinks I'm a loose cannon." Cassie cringed at all the emotional details she'd divulged, flipping the hairdryer on to groom her curly locks.

"He obviously wasn't so put off by your emotional dumping that he didn't want to get in your panties, so I think you're safe. He seemed okay rescuing the damsel in distress. Do you think you guys will see each other again? I mean, after this weekend?" Sarah yelled over the sound of the dryer.

"I think so." Cassie smiled like a college girl who had gotten asked to a fraternity formal. "I mean, he kept saying that he wasn't going to let me go this time."

"Oh, hell. You better get the ball rolling and file for divorce because you know Rick isn't going to do it. He's been texting me nonstop, wanting to know how to get you back. I told him to fuck off, but it didn't work." They both laughed at Sarah's uncharacteristic abrasiveness that was starting to appear more frequently in her conversations with Liz and Rick.

"One thing is for certain: I'm going to see Dylan in about twenty minutes," Cassie confirmed noting her short time frame. She shut off the blow dryer, put the finishing touches on her hair and quickly dabbed on some makeup. The two friends continued to hash out the previous evening's reunion until Cassie had completed her look. She reached her hand out to Sarah, helping her off the bathroom floor.

"I just want you to be happy. Whatever that may look like. You deserve it, baby girl."

———◆———

Cassie was in between a run and a swift trot, heading into the hotel lobby. She rounded the corner, slightly out of breath. Dylan stood by the closed conference room doors holding a cup of coffee. Damn, he looked hot. If she hadn't been out of breath from running, then Cassie would have for sure been puffing hard after laying eyes on him.

"You're late, doc." He smiled, handing her the coffee cup. "I assume you still take it the same way?"

"Yes. Thank you." She straightened her peach sleeveless dress before taking the cup from him. The dress was form fitting to show off her lean figure. She had packed it for last night's dinner, but since she had never made it back to Sarah's to change, she figured she would give Dylan some eye candy for the day. He wasn't shy one bit about staring her down from head to toe before opening the door for her. He pointed to two open seats near the middle of the room and led her to them before she could contest. As they squeaked by the other attendants already in the row, Cassie looked back at Dylan, her eyes shooting daggers.

"Listen. I'm not the one who's late. We don't have many choices," he defended in response to her glare. "I remember you like the back row, end of the aisle seats for a quick midcourse exit. However, let's face it, we aren't as young as we used to be, and neither are my eyes," he whispered as they sat down. "By the way, you look amazing." He leaned in and slid his hand between her thighs. Cassie's pulse quickened and her breathing got heavy. She was so thankful that the room was dark so that the old man sitting next to her didn't notice she was flush. She squeezed Dylan's hand firmly, giving him an easy tiger stare. It was all she could do to focus on nasopharyngeal squamous cell carcinoma for the next few hours. Flashbacks of the previous night's rendezvous clouded her concentration, making the lunch intermission a welcomed event. The swarm of lanyard-clad bodies around long buffet tables made the exit more of a test in their Frogger skills, but somehow Dylan was able to guide them to a clearing.

"You got any protein bars in that thing?" he asked, nodding to her oversized tote as they stood at the back of the buffet line.

"I'm sure I do. You know I don't do hungry very well."

"Good." He grabbed her hand and led her toward the elevator. "I say let's ditch the buffet and have ourselves a unicorn lunch break instead." Cassie smiled hearing the secret code phrase they had created way back when. For years, they had indulged in quick lunch escapes that were the highlight of their med school careers. As a matter of fact, they may have been the only thing that had gotten them through that immensely stressful time in their lives. It seemed like yesterday—him waiting outside her classroom to grab her on her way to do lab work or clinical rounds. She never said no. And she didn't this time either.

Unfortunately, this time they had other passengers on board the elevator, but that didn't stop Cassie from starting the taunting process. As they crammed into the elevator, she made sure to press her backside firmly into Dylan. His warm breath in her ear and firm grip on her hips confirmed that her tactics were working. As they nudged by the other passengers to exit the elevator, making a beeline to their haven, Dylan swung open the door to his room, swiftly grabbing the "Do Not Disturb" sign and hanging it out to display.

"Leave your dress on," he commanded in a tone that made her heart stop. "Take your panties off." Cassie did as she was told. She didn't require a ton of coaxing. She loved being directed by a man. She had been reliving last night's events in her mind all morning in class, so she was primed and ready. With the skills of a professional, he unbuckled his pants and slipped her dress up above her waist as he hoisted her against the wall, pressing into her in one firm thrust. While she missed his warm bare chest against her, there was something erotic about the red power tie tossed across his shoulder as he heaved her up against the hotel wall. It wasn't long before she felt him run his fingers through her hair, gripping her scalp tightly in his fist. As he grabbed her hips, pulling her in closer, she took his well-known cue as they melted deep into each other. Proud smiles covered their faces as they kissed each other and laughed at their efficiency. They scrambled to make themselves presentable once again. His damp, wrinkled shirt and her imperfect, smeared makeup were quickly corrected. Cassie reached into the oversized bag, tossing him a chocolate chip peanut butter protein bar that he retrieved Mr. Miyagi style as he opened the door. They gave each other a quick high five as Cassie strutted past him through the doorway and into the hall with the skills of a well-versed Victoria's Secret runway model. Yes, it was confirmed. Life was full of surprises.

CHAPTER EIGHTEEN

Cassie

A S LUCK WOULD have it, both Sarah and Hal were free from hospital duties that evening. Sarah was chomping at the bit to get her eyes on Dylan. The four of them had decided to meet at City Market for drinks and dinner. The outdoor venue was casual and perfect for an evening of catching up on life.

Cassie and Dylan had taken the ferry once again from the Westin to River Street. On the walk to City Market, Cassie had tried to quickly brief Dylan on Sarah and Hal. Sarah had dated a few guys throughout med school, but none very seriously. She had been laser focused on school and was way tamer with boys than her two room-mates. It would be difficult to even describe a "type" for Sarah. Growing up in rural Kentucky, Sarah's high school boyfriend, and longest relationship until Hal, was a farm boy. Her college dating career consisted of quite the opposite. Sarah had hung out with the hippie-type guys, describing them as "free spirits that didn't want a qualifying term for relationships," which she had been fine with, as her main focus had been getting into med school. Cassie and Dylan tried hard to remember anyone substantial from their time in Atlanta.

"Wasn't there some guy in law school she used to hook up with?" Dylan recounted as they held hands walking the street lined with live oaks and Spanish moss.

"Yes. Reid was his name," Cassie said nodding. "He was

nice, but super quiet and serious."

"Maybe that's why she never brought him around us much. Didn't want us to scare him off," Dylan chuckled.

"Remember the Army guy she met at a bar in Buckhead? I remember him prancing around in our kitchen a few mornings in his tight t-shirts and camo pants," Cassie said with a little sexy growl. Dylan lightly jerked her arm at the comment. Cassie couldn't help but smile at his playful display of jealously. "That's really all I can remember. Of that list, there are no commonalities. It's like a hodge-podge of single male soup."

"You said she and Hal met here in Savannah?"

"Yes. At the hospital. On her first day of work. Hal is a pediatric cardiologist, and one of her first patients was a newborn with a congenital heart defect. They were on the same clinical team. She claims sparks flew the instant they met. She called me and Liz and told us she had finally met her husband. Of course, knowing her lack of interest in most men, we were all ears. The first time I saw them together, I knew she was right. They are perfect. Just wait until you meet him. There they are!" Cassie pointed to Sarah and Hal waving them to the table.

Cassie's stomach flipped a few times over as she and Dylan approached the black wrought iron table that Sarah and Hal had claimed

"*Eek!* Dylan, oh, my goodness. It's so good to see you," Sarah shrieked as she stood on her tippy toes to wrap her arms around his neck.

"You sure are a sight for sore eyes, sweet Sarah." Dylan smiled from ear to ear as he returned the hug. Extending his hand to shake with Hal, Cassie could see how happy Dylan was to be back in the presence of old friends. It was like coming home after years of being away.

City Market was buzzing with live music and half-tipsy locals mixed with fully drunk vacationers as it always was on a Saturday night. A local band played a Stevie Nicks cover as people danced on the brick terrace. The night was gorgeous. The cool breeze paired with Savannah's well-known humidity had fully ignited the curls in Cassie's hair, which had already been amplified earlier in the day from the steam generated during her lunch time high-intensity cardio lovemaking session.

After several rounds of drinks, countless retold old stories that Hal kindly acted amused by, and an entire Vinnie Van Go Go's pizza, they decided to call it a night. Once again, their late evening events had put them out well past the last ferry ride back across the river. Hal, being the responsible one, had stopped drinking well into the evening and offered to drive Dylan back to the hotel in lieu of a taxi. Dylan gratefully accepted Hal's offer, and three of the four of them piled drunkenly into the car as Hal responsibly took the driver's seat. In the backseat, Dylan was as handsy as a teenage boy on a first date. Cassie felt a twinge of sadness as Hal pulled up to the entrance of the hotel. She needed to stay with Sarah tonight. Afterall, she *had* come to the continuing education course upon Sarah's invitation. But Dylan's expectations were clear as he whispered into Cassie's ear, "You're staying with me, right?"

Cassie shook her head no and gave him a *I can't* look. "I'll be just a second, guys," Cassie reassured Hal and Sarah of her intended return as she stepped out of the car with Dylan.

Dylan locked her up tightly in a hug, kissing her neck. "Please, Cassie. Come stay with me."

"I want to, Dylan. I promise. But I can't do that to Sarah. I came here this weekend to spend time with her. While I am more than thankful that I found you here, I owe her at least a nice, long one-on-one breakfast in the morning before I head back to Tampa. You understand, right?"

"You sure are a good friend. You and Sarah are lucky

to have each other." He smiled, pausing before his next words. "Don't mention this to her, but when you got up from the table to grab the pizza with Hal, she threatened my life if I hurt you." Dylan laughed and then a stillness took over his face as he looked at her with eyes filled with sincerity. "Cassie, I know you have been hurt. And I know those wounds are still fresh. But I promise that I would never—could never—hurt you like that. You are the love of my life. You and I both know that. Will you please give me a chance? Again?"

Cassie nodded, fighting back the tears. For the first time in two days with him, she felt vulnerable. She didn't want to leave him. She knew his words were true.

"When can I see you again? I will come to you. Unless you want to get out of Tampa."

"I'm free next weekend," she was somehow able to get out past the lump in her throat. "I have an amazing view from my condo that I would love to show you." She smiled, extending him an invitation.

"I would love to see that. But I can assure you that the most amazing view in the world is staring me in the face right now." Dylan cupped her cheek in his large, strong hand and stroked her lower lip with his thumb. "Stop biting your lip or you won't make it back to the car. You know what that does to me," he whispered in his sexy voice, acknowledging her instinctual nervous habit that always made an appearance when she was trying to stifle her emotions. "I'll talk to you tomorrow night. I want to know you get back home safely," he said as he planted the sweetest goodbye kiss on her lips.

Cassie reluctantly got into the car, looking back at Dylan. There he was, her past, her present, and hopefully her future…all wrapped into one.

CHAPTER NINETEEN

Liz

LIZ'S MIND WAS spinning out of control. More accurately, her *life* was spinning out of control. Her awkward "bump" into Cassie had been playing over and over in her mind. She still had so much she wanted to say, but the deep pain she felt from both Rick and John shutting her out had ignited undue resentment toward her best friend. Her heart and soul were a tangled mess of guilt and jealousy. Liz missed her best friend, and she missed her husband, but she missed her lover too.

John was still out of the house and only speaking to her when he absolutely had to about work or the logistics of the boys as they flip-flopped between the two of them. The house had become so quiet. While her heart broke from missing John's companionship and not seeing her sons every day, what she secretly missed was the way Rick had made her feel. He still hadn't returned any of Liz's calls or texts since he had hung up on her. She knew he wouldn't, but that didn't stop her from hitting the send button. Maybe if she could just catch him in a moment of weakness, she could find her way back into the arms she so desperately craved.

Liz wasn't quite sure how, but she needed to talk to Cassie again soon too. Finding out where Cassie stood with forgiving Rick would be the key to finding how close she would be to getting either her best friend back, or Rick. At this point, she had lost it all. She had nothing more to lose.

Liz found herself sitting in the parking lot of Cassie's high-rise condo. Exactly what she would say when she approached Cassie, she didn't know. And exactly what condo Cassie lived in, well, she didn't know that either. But what she *did* know was that Cassie got home around four on Fridays. After years of meeting up for Friday cocktails after work, Cassie's schedule was easy to decipher.

"What the hell am I doing?" Liz mumbled to herself. "I have turned into a damn stalker." She banged her head against her headrest, feeling like a lunatic. "I'm losing it." Maybe if she hurried, she could get out of the parking lot before running the risk of Cassie seeing her. But as she started to put the car in drive, she noticed Cassie's SUV pulling up with a large black Chevy truck trailing close behind. Luckily, Liz was out of sight. She put her car in park and was so thankful she did because what she proceeded to witness made her body freeze. It was like seeing a ghost from her past. "Dylan?" she whispered to herself. "No fucking way."

Cassie and Dylan got out of their vehicles, unloaded his luggage, and, wrapped up arm-in-arm, they walked into her building. It wasn't until they were out of sight that she kicked herself for not taking a photo.

She had to tell Rick, for so many reasons. First of all, maybe this would help him move on. Secondly, this was her chance to make their taboo affair not appear so immoral. After all, Cassie and Rick were still married. And lastly—and most selfishly—she hoped she would be the one he would turn to for comfort. This was her moment, her one chance, to fix something, anything.

"Dial Rick Buchanon," she voice-commanded to her car. Her heart sank using his real name. The Favorite Mistake contact was useless. There was no need to use his burner number now that the cat was out of the bag, and she assumed Rick had already gotten rid of it by now anyway. But something had kept her from deleting the contact. Nostalgia, maybe? Hope, maybe? She wasn't sure. There was no answer from Rick, of course. Her fingers shook as she texted him.

Rick, please answer me. It's about Cassie. There's something you need to know.

She saw the dots popping up on her phone. He had taken the bait. *What is it? Is she okay?*

Yes, but I need to tell you something. In person. I'm coming over.

He didn't respond, but at least he didn't say no. That was a plus. Her heart raced and her palms started to sweat as her anxiety at physically being in the same room as him rose to an all-time high. She hadn't laid eyes on him since they had been discovered by Cassie. Liz imagined herself embracing him, comforting him in a time of distress. But when she got there, he was cold and stand-offish. While he didn't look a mess like he did the last time she'd seen him, he had lost a significant amount of weight. His face looked hollow and his eyes darker. The golf shirt that had once stretched perfectly over his broad, firm chest now hung loosely from his shoulders, barely touching anything underneath. He motioned for her to come in but remained standing in the kitchen behind the bar. Liz awkwardly took a seat on a barstool, despite him not offering it to her.

"Why do I feel like I'm being tricked? Why are you here?" Rick looked at her with suspicious eyes, placing his hands on his hips.

"Rick, you might want to sit down for this." Liz pulled out the barstool next to her from under the counter.

"No, thanks. I'm fine right where I am. At a safe distance from you."

"Okay. Have it your way then." Liz took a deep breath. The magnitude of the words she was about to tell him were overwhelming. "I decided I wanted to try and speak with Cassie since she too has been avoiding me. The random run-in I had with her recently at the hospital wasn't the ideal way for me to try and apologize. So I drove to her place a few minutes ago and thought I'd wait for her to get home and try to talk to her. I know it sounds stalkerish, but no one seems to be returning my calls or texts lately," Liz proclaimed sarcastically as Rick crossed his arms. "I saw Cassie…" she paused, "and I also saw Dylan."

"Dylan? As in ex-boyfriend from medical school Dylan?" Rick questioned with a furrowed brow.

"Yes. That Dylan. They pulled up at the same time, parked their cars, and walked arm-in-arm into her building, with his luggage in tow."

"Are you sure it was them? This was just a few minutes ago?" Rick started pacing the kitchen floor, running his fingers through his hair.

"Yes, I'm sure I know what Cassie drives and looks like," Liz replied in a snarky tone. "I obviously haven't seen Dylan in a while, but he has fairly distinct features, so I'm about ninety-nine percent sure it was him." Liz started to feel agitated at how panicked and restless Rick was getting as she spoke. Liz watched Rick cover his mouth with his hand, his mind obviously whirling with a game plan. She was hoping for more of an angry or sad response, something she could either fuel or comfort. But instead, she saw desperation. And that just pushed him closer to wanting Cassie back.

"I have to talk to her." Rick reached for his phone on the bar. Liz quickly grabbed his wrist. "Do. Not. Touch. Me, Liz. Do I make myself clear?" Rick's words had fire behind them and, for the first time ever, Liz was a little afraid of him. She released her grip, jumping back, startled at his hateful tone. "You can leave now," he said firmly, pointing to the door.

"I know you're upset. You need to process this before

you talk to her," Liz pleaded. "Maybe she was seeing him all along. Maybe she's happy now, maybe this was all meant to be. Maybe this is your sign to move on."

"Maybe you should mind your own business. Maybe you should focus on your own marriage. And maybe, just maybe, you should accept the fact that I regret ever fucking you at all. If I could take it all back and have my life the way it was before, I would do it so fast, it would make your head spin. Now *go*!" Rick yelled, stomping toward the door, and yanking it wide open. Tears filled Liz's eyes. His words cut her deeper than she believed she could ever survive.

CHAPTER TWENTY

Rick

NO SOONER HAD Liz backed out of the driveway, Rick was backing out of his garage. He knew where he was headed, but he didn't know what he would do when he got there. He had to see Cassie and Dylan with his own eyes to believe it. As he pulled into the parking lot, he could see Cassie's SUV. Next to it sat the big black truck with Georgia tags. It had to be Dylan's. Rick pulled into a spot tucked into the corner and pulled out his cell phone. He dialed Cassie's number over and over. Each time, her voicemail picked up.

"Damn it, answer your phone." Rick only knew one other person that might answer him and that was Sarah.

Sarah, please call me. It's about Cassie. I need to tell you something.

Within seconds, his phone rang.

"This better be legit, Rick. I'm busy at work and I do *not* have time for your desperate measures."

"I'm sorry. But you're the only one that can help me. Cassie won't answer my calls and I need to talk to her right now."

"It's not that she isn't answering. You can call and text all you want, but she's blocked your number. So, you can try and try, but unless you send her a smoke signal, I doubt she'll even know you're trying to reach her. Why are you so desperate to talk to her?"

"I know about Dylan." Rick paused. Even saying his

name made the bile rise into his throat. "I *am* still her husband. I deserve to know what the hell she's doing."

"No, Rick, you actually forfeited all of those rights when you screwed our best friend for months. I'm not sure how you would even know about them unless you're stalking her—which, by the way, is a crime. So, I suggest you leave her alone, because I can promise you, she knows *exactly* what she's doing. And she's happy. Goodbye, Rick."

Sarah was right. He had no place questioning Cassie and her actions right now. But he had to try and win her back, somehow. As he drove away, he felt like a captain bailing on his sinking ship, leaving his marriage to drown without him. He sped quickly toward the marina where he housed his boat. He needed an escape from this nightmare he had created.

The boat raced at lightning speed through the bay as Rick pressed the throttle as far forward as it would go. Salty water crashed around him as the boat jumped and skipped through the air riding the waves. The sun was high and hot and felt blistering against Rick's skin that hadn't seen daylight in who knows how long. The man who had once prided himself on health and fitness had recently been surviving on hard liquor and the occasional sandwich as his source of nutrition. His appetite had completely disappeared, and the very thought of food made him nauseous. He was withering away, physically and emotionally. His days were filled with naps in an eerily silent house and his nights were restless as he tossed and turned in his empty bed, hoping for a miracle that he knew wasn't going to happen.

As he rode the waves through the bay, he wanted so badly to keep heading into the Gulf and never stop. His mind raced with sickening images of Cassie with Dylan. His intuition told him she had always still loved Dylan. He could tell by the way her eyes lit up whenever Liz had mentioned his name in an old story. But he'd never dreamed that she would be back in his arms before her tears had dried over their marriage. He had no one to blame but himself for their reunion, though. Cassie had warned Rick that for her, trust was the biggest necessity in a relationship. Her words rang loudly in his mind as he recounted the number of times that she told him that being unfaithful was a deal breaker. That there would be no second chances. He knew the first time he made love to Liz that he had crossed a line he could never jump back over. But at the time, the spontaneity and excitement had overshadowed the repercussions. The electricity he'd once felt while thinking of Liz had now turned to sinking feelings of regret.

Rick eyed Cassie's high-rise in the distance. His heart sank, thinking about how much she had always wanted to live on the bay. *Why didn't I just give her what she wanted? Sure, a house on Bayshore was expensive and didn't make for the most private space, but what would it have mattered in the long run if it would have made her happy?* Regret thickened in his heart as the tall, white building crept closer into his view. Slowing the throttle, he stared up at the black-railed balconies. She was in one of those condos. With Dylan. His heart ached at the thought. Reaching down into the glove compartment, he pulled out his binoculars. He had reached desperation mode and he didn't care. As he scanned the balconies and windows for any sign of Cassie, he thought he caught a glimpse of her blonde hair about ten stories up. With the boat still jumping over the waves, Rick found it hard to focus on what he thought might be Cassie. Overwhelmed with frustration and helplessness, Rick screamed at the top of his lungs. He fell to his knees and rolled onto his back on the bow of the boat, staring up to the clouds. He felt small and broken. As the white forms swirled above him into ambiguous shapes, he realized he wasn't in control. Tears streamed from his eyes and dripped into his ears, and, for the first time in a long time, he prayed. He prayed for a miracle and for forgiveness. And with his whole heart, he prayed for another chance to love Cassie.

CHAPTER TWENTY-ONE

Cassie

SEEING DYLAN IN her space, in her world, was magnificent. Cassie uncorked the bottle of expensive red wine she had been saving for something extra special. She happened to be staring at that "something extra special" as he walked onto her balcony. Dylan appeared larger than life, almost majestic, his hands grasping the rails of the balcony while the sunset draped over his broad shoulders. His head shifted left to right as he scanned the view, his salt and pepper hair now messy from the breeze as it whipped off the bay. As she carried the two partially-filled glasses out to him, he turned to her, and very slowly and intentionally took them out of her hands, placing them on the glass-top table. Leaning down close to her face, he planted a warm kiss on her hand, and then her cheek, then her neck, and finally, with their gazes locked, her lips.

"I missed you this week." She smiled up at him, pulling him in close to her.

"I've missed you for a decade," he rebutted.

"Always trying to one-up me, eh?" She handed him his glass, raising hers for a toast. "I would like to propose a toast…but there's one condition."

"What's that?"

"You have to look me directly in the eyes as we toast. I heard from a friend recently that if you toast someone without looking at them intentionally as your wine glasses touch, you will be cursed with bad sex for a year."

"Yikes, now *that's* a curse. But you and I both know that isn't possible with us." He winked as he raised his glass, the delicate red wine spinning in the large vessel.

"True. But let's be safe, just in case. To us—our past, present, and future." Cassie's eyes didn't leave his as their glasses touched, probably a little too forcefully. Dylan bugged his eyes out at her in an exaggerated effort to make sure Cassie noted their place locked in her gaze, leading both of them to laughter as they drank to the toast. As they curled up on the outdoor sofa to watch the sunset's grand finale before it ducked behind the horizon, Cassie couldn't imagine anywhere she would rather be.

Her perfectly serene setting was quickly interrupted by the sound of pings coming from her phone. She desperately wanted to ignore them but being a physician had as many negatives as perks. Having to be available to the hospital and patients at almost all times was definitely one of the downsides. To her surprise, it wasn't the hospital or the office call center.

"Who is it, Cas? The hospital?" Dylan could see the concern on her face as she read the words.

"No. I hate to say it, but I wish it were. It's Sarah. She got a call from Rick. He knows you're here."

"So? Does that really matter? Wait," he paused, changing his tone from annoyed to empathetic. "I'm sorry, Cassie. I should be more sensitive to your situation. This probably makes you a little uncomfortable." He stroked her hair to comfort her. "Have you heard from him? How would he know?" Dylan questioned.

"I wouldn't know if he's been trying to reach me. I blocked his number. His relentless texts and voicemails were causing me so much anxiety, I had no choice. I've only seen or spoken to him once, and that was when I went back to our house to get my things. I made it very clear that I wanted nothing to do with him. What if he's having me followed?"

"Have you started the divorce process? Not that I'm a professional at divorces, but I do have friends who have been through a few doozies, and they sometimes used private investigators to build a case against their spouse for financial or child custody purposes."

"He can have everything we own. And thankfully we don't have children," Cassie said with disgust. It was the first time she could remember being relieved she hadn't gotten pregnant. "I don't want anything that he or Liz have touched...ever. I met with an attorney last week. The separation papers are being drafted. I have spent this entire week gathering financial documents. Dylan, this could get really ugly. Are you sure you want to get in the middle of this? I will totally understand if you want to wait until the dust settles for us to see each other." Cassie spoke genuinely.

"Cassie," Dylan was firm in his tone. "There is nothing that scares me more than being *without* you. An angry, cheating ex-husband is nothing compared to that. And I mean that with all that I have. You're not going to do this alone." He squeezed her hand and lifted her chin up to meet his stare. She believed him.

"So, I guess we get to hang out in my condo for the next few days on lockdown. Hope you like delivery food. The thought of Rick spying on us or confronting us together is something I just can't handle right now. I need to find out more before we go out in public around here. Is that okay?"

"I would eat pizza and Chinese food for weeks if it meant I got to be holed up with you. Don't worry about me. I'm easy to please." He smiled, slipping his hand between her thighs. Cassie's heart burst. She threw her long legs across his lap, straddling the ridiculously attractive man. It felt so good to trust someone again.

"Thank you. I'm not sure what I did to deserve another

chance with you, but I will take the opportunity and run before anyone changes their mind." And she pushed down firmly onto him with her hips engaging his. As the sunset wrapped up its show, their very own lovemaking episode began.

———◆———

As the sunlight crept through the cracks in the blinds, Cassie felt Dylan's hand brush across her forehead, sweeping the mess of blonde waves from her face.

"Good morning, sweetheart. I made you some breakfast." The smell of cinnamon and coffee filled the room as he placed the plate of French toast and eggs over her lap. Her heart beamed at the sweet gesture. "I figured you needed the breakfast of champions after last night. You need to refuel." Dylan snickered as he sat down beside her on the bed and kissed her cheek.

"We must have tried to make up for lost time all in one night. I can't remember the last time I had that many orgasms, but since you were dishing them out, I was happy to take them." Cassie smiled, taking a big sip of coffee. She had always remembered him to be an incredible lover, but time had a way of blurring memories, even the most vivid and intense ones. She was elated having had her memory refreshed and had acquired an even greater appreciation for his skills after the previous night's performance.

"What happened to us? Why did we quit? I honestly cannot remember. Do you?" Dylan asked candidly. "I have played our relationship over again and again in my mind. I can't for the life of me put my finger on why we ended. We loved each other then, and we love each other now." Dylan's eyes were soft and gentle. Cassie was a little taken aback at the bold topic first thing in the morning.

"Wow. Can I at least finish my coffee before the heavy conversations?" She laughed, took a sip, and then proceeded to answer his questions. "I think we were young, and we didn't know what we had. I think we were focused on our careers. And I think we were tired and stressed from school. As much as we loved, we also fought. I'm sure you haven't forgotten our knock-down, drag-out fights." She raised her eyebrows and popped her fork loaded with syrupy French toast into her mouth.

"Funny you say that. I can't remember why we fought. But I definitely remember us making up." Dylan winked at her.

"Why am I not shocked? Let me remind you, dear. Do you remember when you bought your first house in Atlanta?"

"Yes. The cute little starter home over in the Vinings." Dylan nodded with nostalgia.

"Do you remember who helped you buy that house?"

"I think my mom went with me that day. Or maybe it was Dad." Dylan's eyes narrowed, trying to remember the details.

"It was your mother. Do you know why I remember?" Cassie inquired as Dylan shook his head no. "Because it was supposed to be me." Dylan looked puzzled, urging Cassie to explain further. "We were nearing the end of our residencies. I still had one year left on my lease with Liz and Sarah. You were going to buy what would be our first home together. As soon as we were done with school and had secured our first jobs, we were going to get engaged and move in together."

"Yes, it's coming back to me now," Dylan nodded, acknowledging her account of the memory, but still not following the magnitude of its purpose.

"I had rotations, but you had found this stellar house that you feared wouldn't be on the market long. I told you to go scope it out and if you liked it, we could go back the next day and put in an offer together, since it would be our first home. You agreed that it was some-

thing we should do as a couple. Then do you remember
what happened?" Cassie asked, feeling the pain well up
inside her just as it had years ago. Dylan shook his head
innocently. "You called me while I was still at the hospital
that evening to tell me you had put an offer in on the
house that day. You said your mom had asked to go with
you at the last minute, and she urged you to press ahead
with an offer because the house was so perfect it would
sell quickly. So, you did. Without me."

"Oh. Yeah. I do remember that now," Dylan whispered
in a remorseful tone.

"That was such a huge indicator to me of what my
future would look like. I never felt *first* our entire relationship. There was always a surgery, an exam, a fishing
tournament, a family event, or anything else but me. You
were sweet to include me in whatever you were doing,
even though all of your hobbies weren't my cup of tea,
like the deer hunting expedition." They both laughed at
that memory. "But I just needed to know that I was your
number one priority. I needed to know that if push came
to shove, you would choose me above all else."

"Cassie, I'm so sorry. It's been a long time and I don't
remember all of the details, but you aren't the only
woman to tell me those exact words. I know my faults.
But I have had years since then to learn to do better.
Please," he begged, lifting her face high to meet his, "you
have to believe me when I tell you that I have my priorities straight now. Let me prove it to you."

"I'm not sure why, but I do believe you. Don't make
me out to be a fool, okay?"

"Cassie, I would be the fool to lose you again. I've
wanted to call you so many times over the years just to
hear your voice and check on you." Dylan propped up
on his elbow so that his eyes were level with hers. "There
hasn't been a day that's gone by that I haven't thought
about you in some way, whether it was an inside joke

I'm reminded of, or a phrase you used to say, or a surgical decision that I wish I had your input on. I can only
assume that it wasn't your ideal plan to go through what
you have with your marriage, but for my sake, I'm glad
Rick fucked up so I get a redo." Dylan leaned in to kiss
her. "Yum." He licked his lips, cleaning off the syrup he
just picked up from hers.

ping. Just as Dylan went for another syrup-smothered
kiss, Cassie's phone alert went off. Reaching over to grab
it, her heart stopped seeing the notification. She quickly
deleted the event from her calendar and focused back on
her coffee and French toast.

"Sweetheart, what's wrong? Are you okay?"

"Um, yeah. It was just a reminder of a doctor's appointment on Monday...with my fertility doctor." She
chugged the coffee, happy it wasn't steaming hot. "I obviously won't be needing that," she stated matter-of-factly.

"Oh. So, you were trying to get pregnant?" Dylan
asked softly.

"Yep. But everything happens for a reason and I'm so
thankful that I never got pregnant. I can't imagine going
through all of this while expecting or having a small
child."

"Yeah. Things work out the way they should most
times, I guess." Dylan paused, not sure how far to pry
into the subject. "So how long had you been trying, if
you don't mind me asking?"

"I don't mind you asking. It used to be harder to talk
about because of the pain of not getting pregnant, but
these days, the pain of my husband sleeping with my best
friend far outweighs that, so it's much easier to talk about.
We had been trying for a couple of years. We spent our
first few years of marriage having fun and traveling. I was
busy at work and I wanted to be stable and prepared. You
know me, Mrs. Perfection. After two years with no luck,
we decided to see a specialist. We figured it was his work

travel schedule or my work stress level. But now looking back on it, I think it just wasn't meant to be."

"Do you still want to have kids?" Dylan asked.

"Of course," she sighed, "but not the way I did it before. I know Rick did a horrible thing, but truthfully, I can see why he was compelled to do what he did." Dylan looked at her with discernment. "You know how driven and how Type A I am, but you ain't seen nothin' 'til you've seen me on fertility hormones with a baby on the agenda." They both laughed. "Rick was microman-aged down to his diet, his vitamins, his sleep patterns, and even his underwear size. I had every pregnancy app perfected with charts and ovulation graphs galore. Every minute of our sex life was on a schedule. There was an agenda, by God, and I was going to make it happen." Cassie pounded her fist into her hand mimicking a judge with a gavel.

"I can only imagine," Dylan said. "But that still didn't give him the right to cheat."

"No, it didn't. But it did break our intimacy. Sex, while it was still good and loving, was a chore sometimes, not something to show love or affection. So, if I ever have the chance again to be a mom, it's going to be organically. If it's meant to be, it will be. I can't risk having the dream of a child breaking up a marriage again."

"That makes sense." Dylan squeezed her hand. "We talked about having kids. Do you remember that?"

Cassie smiled. "Of course. That's why I'm shocked that you never married and had any."

"I could have. But it just wasn't right. It never felt right. I agree with you that if things are meant to be, then they happen usually with no force or pressure. Endurance, yes. But force, no."

Cassie paused as she digested Dylan's words. They made so much sense to her. All the years she'd spent with Rick trying to get pregnant she had presumed were displays of endurance. She'd believed that if she stood strong and prayed hard enough, that someday it would be her turn. But after hearing his words, she realized she'd had it wrong all along. She had been forcing it with all her might. And eventually, something had to give from the pressure…her marriage. As she looked at Dylan, Cassie realized that they, in fact, were the epitome of endurance. In that moment, she had no sadness, no fatigue, no resentment. Just pure relief in having him by her side.

"Speaking of endurance, you must be refueled by now." Dylan grabbed the tray of food from her lap and placed it on the floor. Gliding his arms under her, he lifted her up and carried her to the bathroom. "How about some hot shower sex?"

"Sounds perfect," Cassie replied, grateful for the spontaneity and pressure-free aspect of their intimacy. As the hot water rushed over them, his fingers ran firmly through her hair. Cold chills raced down her spine. Cassie's lips were in heaven as they kissed his wet shoulders.

Dylan lathered up soap and slowly began to wash her, his fingers tracing her shoulders. As he swept down her arms, he stopped at her hands. Massaging her palms one at a time, Cassie could feel years of stress leaving her body. Her hands were her lifeline as a surgeon, and they rarely got any love. Leave it to Dylan to know just what she needed. His hands slid around her breasts, purposefully avoiding them, with a straight line to her hips. Cassie smiled at his tease. His hands traveled to her inner thighs. As her breathing got heavy, she could feel his heart beating through his chest as her head rested on him. Turning her around to face the shower wall, he swept her hair over her shoulders and, with firm pressure, massaged them. Tracing her vertebrae with his thumbs, his hands finally made their way to her breasts. As his lips kissed the back of her neck, she was drenched in warmth both inside and out, and there wasn't a sensation he was igniting that she ever wanted to forget. Overcome with emotion, tears streamed down her face. He felt so good. She was so thankful for their endurance. But more than anything, she was indebted to the shower for masking the sight of her tears. She wasn't sure if she could put her feelings into words if he pried at the cause of them. Luckily, she didn't have to. As she pressed back hard into him, her emotions were muted as they both succumbed to pleasure.

———◆———

Their weekend on lockdown had turned into a blessing in disguise. Getting to reconnect and catch up after years of being apart was icing on the cake to being able to feel his closeness again. Cassie had forgotten how much she loved talking to Dylan, even over meaningless things. She had especially missed the sound of his contagious laugh.

She realized during the course of the day that he hadn't seen John yet.

"Why didn't you and John keep in touch over the years? You guys were so close in school."

"Well, let's face it. You and Liz were inseparable, and John and I were along for the ride. Once you and I broke up, I was the one kicked off the island. I didn't want to cause any friction between John and Liz, so I let it go. Plus, guys are different than girls about keeping up with friendships."

With that, Cassie decided to surprise Dylan and have John over for dinner that evening. Cassie hadn't seen him since they'd both been at Sarah's, and she wanted to check in on him to make sure he was doing okay. He seemed to be doing as well as could be expected from their brief text messages, but those could be deceiving.

John's patented three-tap knock made its debut on the sleek mahogany door. Cassie turned to see Dylan's eyebrows furrow at the unexpected guest.

"You expecting someone?" Dylan asked as he headed to answer the door.

"I took the liberty of ordering us takeout for dinner. Hope that's okay. Do you mind grabbing the door for me?" she called from the kitchen as she grabbed a bottle of wine. She wasn't completely lying. It was a version of the truth. Cassie stood back and watched with butterflies of excitement while Dylan grabbed the chrome door handle and opened it. She couldn't wait to see his face when he laid eyes on John.

"John?" Dylan belted out, part scream, part laugh. "Man, what a great surprise!" Dylan stuck his large hand out to grasp John's in a firm handshake as he welcomed him into the condo. "Cas, did you arrange this?" Dylan asked as he took the carryout bags from John's grasp.

"No, babe. I had no idea that John was now an Uber Eats driver." She chuckled as she whisked her arms around John's neck, kissing him on the cheek.

"I figured I'll need a second job after Liz takes all of my money in a divorce pretty soon," John said sarcastically, playing along with Cassie's antics.

"Well, you're definitely the most well-dressed, educated food delivery person I have ever seen." Dylan smoothed over the awkwardness of John's questionable marital status as he played along as well.

"Dylan, you seriously haven't changed a bit. How have you been? It's been way too long." Cassie handed John and Dylan each a large glass of cabernet and waved them onto the balcony. The wind coming off the bay made for a perfect temperature. It would have been considered muggy and hot if it wasn't for the breeze. Bamboo hurricane lanterns protected lit candles from being extinguished while the flames danced from the remnants of wind that snuck through. Anita Baker was playing a slow tune on the speaker and the outdoor table was set for a party of three with white melamine plates and fine linen napkins adorned with a tropical print. "Cassie tells me you have a stalker on your hands," John began after taking a big sip of wine.

"Man, I didn't realize what a sketchy love triangle we had going on here. The dynamics of this situation have definitely been something from a daytime TV show."

"Fucked up, isn't it? Run while you still can, bro." John jokingly motioned to the door. Cassie listened to the two men catch up on life and business as she unpacked the perfectly grilled steaks onto the crisp, white plates. She heard John start to open his conversation up to the elephant in the room—Liz. Cassie could tell by his unabbreviated dialogue that he really needed and wanted to talk about the past few weeks. As the wine continued to flow, so did the details of the topic.

"Did you have any clue?" Dylan asked John cautiously.

"Not an inkling. I knew she was struggling with sadness and insecurities, but I thought it was just a mid-life crisis or something. I never in a million years dreamed she would cheat on me. In our entire relationship, I had never even *considered* being with another woman. I guess I was naïve to think that she felt the same way. Cassie, have you heard from Liz?"

"I wouldn't know. I blocked both her and Rick from my phone. I would have never known Rick was aware of Dylan being here if it hadn't been for him calling Sarah. My attorney said to make sure all correspondence with him is kept to a minimum and that if I need to communicate, it should be through email since that will create a paper trail. That recommendation was fine by me. The sound of his voice or the sight of his name popping up on my phone makes me nauseous, so I was happy to block him. I'm so glad he had the nerve to call Sarah. I can't imagine being caught off guard if he had been able to approach me and Dylan."

"You don't think he's dangerous, do you?" Dylan asked,

concerned.

"No, not at all," Cassie reassured him. "He's desperate and ruthless enough to do away with his pride and beg for my forgiveness, but not enough to physically hurt anyone. John, have you decided what you're going to do about your marriage? Has Liz said anything about trying to reconcile?"

"I wish I had an answer, Cas. I'm so tired of living out of a suitcase in short-term rentals. We really haven't even talked at all except for work or kid logistics."

"Speaking of the boys, how are Paul and Sam handling the situation?" Cassie asked sincerely.

"Surprisingly, they haven't seemed to miss a beat. You know, over the years they have always had to adapt and go with the flow. With either Liz, myself, or both of us always being at the hospital, they've become accustomed to hopping between nannies, grandparents, friend's parents, etc. Ironically, I think it was the perfect training for this situation. Liz and I both agreed to keep most of the details of the separation to a minimum. They don't need to know them anyway. As much as I resent Liz for her actions, I still want our sons to see their mother as respectable.

"John, you're a better man than me. I would have already packed up for good and made my way to have an intense conversation with Rick," Dylan said.

"What good would that do? She's just as much at fault as he is. Besides, Rick's real punishment is living the rest of his life without Cassie." John smiled at his friend. "And we all know he's already experiencing the hell of regret."

"I must admit, as selfish as it sounds, I'm glad I get to reap the rewards of his stupidity." Dylan grabbed Cassie's thigh under the table and squeezed it firmly. She felt her heart skip a beat. Something about his touch could stop her in her tracks. As she sat there staring at the candle-light reflecting off his skin, the world seemed imperfectly perfect. The road to healing her heart and piecing her life back together wouldn't be short or easy, but she had a good man to help her along the way. As the last bit of wine was poured and the night came to a close, the three old friends laughed at how random and ironic life had turned out to be. And they vowed to make it through the crazy ride together, just like old friends always do.

CHAPTER TWENTY-TWO

Cassie

"DO YOU *HAVE* to go? Can't you wait another hour? Please…" Cassie begged as Dylan folded his clothes and packed them away in his suitcase. "I can make it worth your while," she taunted, giving him her best sexy wink and lip bite.

"Babe, you know I would give anything to stay longer, but I have a surgery first thing in the morning and it's a five-hour drive from here." Dylan wrapped his arms around her waist, pulling her in close and burying his face in her blonde curls.

"I hate Monday morning surgeries. You need to train your scheduler better than that," she grumbled, wrapping her leg around him and wrestling him onto the bed.

"Cas, Brunswick, Georgia is definitely *not* Tampa, Florida. We don't have nearly as many operating rooms as you do. So you have to take what you can get when you can get it." Dylan brushed the hair back from her face as she straddled him, leaning down to kiss him.

"Well, then, that's one more reason you need to move to a bigger city like this."

"Oh, you think so, do you? Well, maybe I can make that happen. Someday. But you never know. What if you like my little slice of beach heaven in Georgia? You haven't even seen it yet. How do you know you won't want to come to me instead?"

"I guess anything is possible. How's the shopping there?

Any really cute boutiques? And besides, it might be nice to get away from all the drama with Rick. The daily fear of running into Liz at the hospital is starting to get old too. As if work isn't stressful enough, now I have to try and watch out for my husband's mistress at every turn. It's exhausting." Cassie dramatically threw herself onto the bed with arms and legs spread out like a snow angel. Dylan rolled his eyes at her acting display.

"Why don't you come check out St. Simon's next weekend? We won't have to be on lockdown all weekend, and I can show you around the island. Think of it as a romantic beach getaway." Dylan's eyes lit up as he proposed the idea.

"I would love to, but I'm on call all next weekend. Can we do the following one?"

"Yuck. I have to wait two weeks to see you?"

"'Tis the life of two doctors trying to save the world. But are you sure you want me to come there? Are you ready to get rid of your single guy reputation? I'm sure it's a small island. You know how people like to talk in small towns. Especially when it comes to the hot, single ENT surgeon."

"Cassie, I couldn't care less what anyone thinks. Besides, any man would be proud to show you off and have you on his arm. I'll make all the plans. Just bring some beach clothes and swimsuits." Dylan jumped up and zipped his suitcase.

A few minutes later, as they approached his truck, her heart sank deep into her stomach. She dreaded seeing him go. He tossed his luggage into the cab and turned to her with a sincere smile.

"Come here," Dylan whispered, pulling her in close to him. She hugged him tightly.

"I think my arms are stuck. I can't let go," she teased.

"Looks like you'll have to go with me then. It will make for an awkward surgery tomorrow, though. I don't

think they make surgical scrubs for conjoined twins."
They both laughed at the thought of that scenario.

"Be safe, Dylan. Thank you for an amazing weekend."

"I'll call you when I get back," he promised, giving her
a goodbye kiss.

Cassie made her way back to the front doors of the
high-rise and turned one last time to give him a goodbye
wave and see his taillights disappear. Once on the lobby
elevator, she nearly skipped as she flipped back through
the album of memories from the weekend. Just as the
elevator doors were about to close, a man's hand forced
them to sling back open. Cassie's breathing stopped as
she saw Rick's face. His eyes were red, his hair a mess,
and his skin pink from the sun. She froze. The doors
closed behind him as he stepped onto the elevator, and
she began to panic.

"What are you doing, Rick? You need to leave this
instant."

"Cassie, I just want to talk to you. I didn't mean to
startle you, but you won't return my calls or texts. I had
no other choice," Rick pleaded.

"We're *over*. There's nothing you can say or do to make
me feel differently. I told you from day one of our marriage, that trust was my number one requirement in a
relationship. And you broke that rule in the most despi-
cable way."

She breezed by him as the elevator doors opened onto
her floor. She could hear his footsteps following her
down the hall and her heart raced with fear. She had
never been so uncomfortable in the presence of a man
she once trusted with her entire world. As she reached
the mahogany door, she looked back to see Rick standing behind her.

"What? Haven't I made myself clear?" she yelled, hoping that someone would hear her and come see what the
commotion was about. She started to wonder what he

might be capable of in his current state of mind.

"I know about Dylan. I know he was here all week-end." Rick's voice cracked as the words came out.

"And why is that any of your business?" She stood with her arms crossed, glaring at him, trying not to let on how nervous he was making her.

"Because you're technically still my wife. And I love you." Rick stepped closer to her, pinning her up against her door. His hands cupped her face and as he leaned in to kiss her. She could smell alcohol on his breath. Cassie pushed him away as hard as she could, and he stumbled backward.

"No! Get off me! I won't be your wife for much longer. I filed for divorce. You'll be getting the papers this week. Now leave or I will call the police."

"What? You filed for divorce? Please, Cassie. Don't…" Rick begged as he took a step toward her once more.

"Go! Now! I mean it Rick." Cassie yelled grabbing her phone from her back pocket to dial for help.

"Okay," Rick whispered in defeat, waving his hands in surrender. "I'll go. But I really do love you, Cassie, and I am so, so sorry for what I did."

Cassie nodded and quickly sought refuge in her condo, closing and locking the door firmly behind her. Leaning against the door, her heart raced, and tears filled her eyes as she melted to the floor. Burying her head into her knees, she sat there, shaking and weeping. She wanted Dylan. She needed him to hold her and make her feel safe. In all their years of marriage, Cassie had never felt threatened by Rick. But she had also never seen him desperate and drunk. She knew if she called Dylan, he would turn back around. He couldn't be far. He probably hadn't even made it to the interstate yet. She desperately wanted to believe that Rick was harmless. And the last thing she wanted was to ignite an altercation between the two of them.

So instead of calling Dylan, she did the only thing that she could think of to move the situation along. Scrolling through the emails on her phone, she found the one she was looking for from Friday. There, in big bold letters in the subject, was the title, "Separation Documents." It had felt wrong opening it with Dylan there. But Cassie couldn't open it fast enough now. Without hesitation, she approved and signed them, giving the go ahead to her attorney to deliver them as soon as possible. A wave of relief rushed over her as she hit the send button.

Cassie made her way onto the balcony for some fresh air. Never in a million years would she have dreamed that she would be in this scenario. It all seemed so surreal. But she had made the best decisions she could with the shitty hand of cards she had been dealt. And while it wasn't the fairy tale ending with Rick that she had imagined, Cassie believed there was still a happy-ever-after waiting for her.

CHAPTER TWENTY-THREE

Liz

LIZ HAD COME to the realization that the only way she would be able to have any sort of communication with anyone involved in this shit-show love-saga was to confront them face-to-face. She had tried several times over the weekend to get in touch with John, so after the silent treatment extended into Sunday, she figured she might have a chance of catching him at the office. After all, she knew his tendency was to drown himself in work when he was in any sort of mental turmoil. She had spotted his car in the parking garage, confirming her hunch at his location. Stepping through the rear entrance to the hospital, Liz was taken aback at how quiet it was in the sterile hallways. The hospital seemed uncharacteristically slow for a weekend. Liz knew it was Kelly's turn to be on call. She had been hoping Kelly would be out making rounds so that she could catch John alone. But as she approached the corridor leading to their office, she could hear a female voice. Liz couldn't help herself. She tiptoed quietly to the edge of the doorway, listening to the conversation that echoed into the hallway.

"Hey, John, you know I'm okay here by myself, right? I had a few hiccups the weekend you were in Charleston, but I think that was new girl jitters. You trust me here alone to handle your patients, right?" Liz could hear Kelly quizzing John.

"Of course. I'm only here because I need to get caught

up on all of these chart notes while I have the time. I promise I have full confidence in you." Liz felt a twinge of jealously at how sweet and reassuring John's tone was toward Kelly.

"I realize it's not my place, but are you and Liz okay? I sense some tension in the office, and I want to make sure it's nothing I've caused." Kelly continued. Liz's heartrate raced wondering what John's response would be and how much information he would divulge to their associate.

"Kelly," John replied softly, "you have to believe me when I tell you that you are the best. We wouldn't have hired you if we didn't believe that fully. And yes, Liz and I are in a rough spot, but I promise it has nothing to do with you." Liz couldn't hold back any longer.

"Ahem," Liz let out a fake cough as she made her way to the office doorway, firing a discerning glare at the two of them holding hands. "Sorry. Am I interrupting something?" Liz asked with anything but an apologetic tone.

"Oh, hey, Liz," Kelly replied, pulling back her hand from John's grasp. Kelly's mortified facial expression revealed that if she could have found a small hole to weasel into, she would have desperately tried to use it as an escape route. John appeared unfazed by Liz witnessing what could have easily been misconstrued as an intimate moment.

"What do you need, Liz?" John questioned with little enthusiasm and a hint of annoyance.

"Could you please give us a moment?" Liz asked Kelly firmly, almost making it an order. Liz shot John a look to kill. He responded to her silent slap with a fuck-off smile. Kelly nodded to her and scurried past Liz standing guard in the doorway as she briskly exited the awkward encounter.

"Even if what you just saw had any more substance to it than a friend comforting another friend, I think *you* of all people should be the last person to judge my actions.

What do you want, Liz?" John huffed.

"You won't answer my calls so I figured maybe I could catch you here. Paul has a soccer tournament coming up. I'm on call here at the office that weekend, so will you be able to take the boys? If not, I need to make other arrangements."

"That should be fine. And the boys can always call me themselves. Paul has a phone."

"John, let's try and act like civil parents and not put our children in the middle of this," Liz retorted.

"Excuse me, but *you* are the one that put us in this situation. Before you decided to screw your best friend's husband, our kids had a loving and supportive home. So don't cast stones at me, *dear.*"

He was right. But she wasn't about to let him see her waver. Liz stood tall and turned to leave, coldly replying to his comment. "I'll have Paul text you with the details on the tournament."

Seeing John touching Kelly, even if it had been inno-cent, ignited a wick of anger so fierce she thought she might explode before she could get to her car. Her feet pounded heavily on the concrete as her mind raced, pic-turing John's grasp on Kelly's hand. She slammed the car door hard as she plopped into the driver's seat. She let loose a bloodcurdling wail as her fists pounded onto the steering wheel in an adult-sized temper tantrum. She accidentally caught the edge of her car horn, causing it to blare loudly above her cry. The alarming sound startled her, causing her to stop dead in her tracks, as she realized how out of control she felt.

"You have lost your fucking mind, Liz," she said to herself, still breathless from her childish display of rage. And to make matters worse, she had no one to confide in. She had been all but ostracized by her two best friends who, in any normal circumstance, would have been her go-to confidants, ready to analyze the predicament with a fine-tooth comb and talk her off of any ledge she may have been teetering on. She had never felt so alone. As she reached to start her car, she heard her phone start to buzz. She froze as she saw the name that popped up on the screen.

"Rick?" she answered, leery that there must be something wrong or some catch as to why he would be calling her. He had made it very clear that he wanted nothing to do with her ever again.

"Hey. I, um, I need to see you." He sounded disoriented and distracted.

"Rick, are you okay? I thought you wished death upon me. Sorry, but I'm a little confused here," Liz replied suspiciously.

"Never mind. I shouldn't have called."

Liz caught him as he was about to hang up. "No, wait!" she yelled. "I'm headed to my house. The boys are with friends for the evening. Just meet me there." Rick didn't respond. Liz simply heard silence as she stared at her phone in confusion realizing he had ended the call. What did he want? Why his sudden need to see her? She didn't care what his exact reasons were. She needed a friend. And if *he* was that person, then she would take it, despite the black cloud that surrounded their relationship.

Liz pulled into her garage. Across the street, Rick sat in his car. Her heart pounded at the thought of being in the same room as him. After he had gotten so enraged with her when she had told him about Dylan, she figured he would never speak to her again, much less want to see her. Liz stood nervously in her kitchen, waiting for him to follow her in, her hands sweating and shaking from apprehension. Something was off with him; she could tell in the tone of his voice over the phone. And when she saw the expression on his face as he made his way through the back door, her suspicion was confirmed. Rick was certainly not himself. His face was beet red from the sun and his eyes were just about the same shade of bloodshot. He didn't say a word as he approached her, pushing her up against the cabinets, pressing himself firmly onto her. As he grabbed her head, pulling her to his lips, Liz smelled alcohol on his breath. He must have been on his boat, drinking, given the sunburn on his face.

"Rick, what are you doing?"

"What does it look like, Liz? Isn't this what you want? Me? Us?" He didn't stop his process as he answered her. Pulling her shirt up and off, he slid her bra straps off her shoulders, exposing her bare chest to him. Liz felt a flood of emotions. Of course, she had been craving Rick's touch, but now he seemed vile, spiteful. Despite her hesitation, she let him continue as he dropped both their pants to the ground. She pulled him in close while he roughly grabbed at her body. There were no words, no eye contact, only a primal rush of movement that seemed to be backed by an agenda. Liz needed closeness, though, even if it came from her dysfunctional extramarital lover. She tried hard to comfort Rick, hoping she could change his frame of mind. She stroked his cheek and grabbed his hand in a tight grip, trying to connect with him like she usually could. But he was cold. As their bodies eventually slowed to a complete stop after he had crudely completed his task, Rick's eyes finally made their way to Liz's and she saw way more than she wanted to see. She saw a broken man swallowed by a sea of pain. The rose-colored glasses she had been wearing for months were finally gone. She wanted nothing more than for him to leave and never be that close to her again. He was a stranger, and she longed for the safety of her husband. Why hadn't she seen this before now? Their entire affair had been a bandage for their individual brokenness, crafted out of lust.

The two of them didn't speak a word as he dressed himself, not even slightly changing his demeanor. Rick let the back door slam closed behind him. Liz slid down to the floor. As she sat there, still naked, knees to her chest, she felt dirty. It was so clear to her what had just transpired: Rick was seeking revenge for Cassie's new love affair with Dylan. Liz couldn't blame him. Afterall, she didn't stop him. She was just as guilty in her actions, yearning for his touch and seeking refuge from isolation. Flooded with regret, Liz became overwhelmed with an intense desire to make things right. She wasn't sure exactly how she would do it, but she had a huge mess to clean up. And she was desperate to find a way to make that happen.

CHAPTER TWENTY-FOUR

Cassie

THE GOLDEN ISLES were just that: golden. As Cassie crossed over the causeway bridge onto St. Simon's Island, she had to make sure not to veer off out of her lane as she tried to soak up every aspect of the view. Blue water was broken into pieces by bits of bright gold marsh grass that danced with the tide. Boats filled with avid fishermen jumped across the waves, leaving streaks of white caps behind them. Cassie could smell the marshy, salty air as it rushed in through her open sunroof. An overwhelming sense of peace and calm made the corners of her lips turn up as she pulled onto the quaint island. Palmetto bushes and palm trees were wedged underneath Georgia pines, and quaint mom-and-pop shops lined the streets. Bikers and walkers were sprinkled on the sidewalks like confetti with their brightly-colored beach apparel and flip flops. Dylan was right: this was nothing like South Tampa, with its highly-polished and manicured women and perfectly-sleek men dressed like GQ models. This island felt cozy and easy.

As she turned onto Dylan's street, she spotted him standing at the edge of his drive. The house was adorable and the yard perfectly maintained. Navy blue hurricane shutters draped the windows on the white wood siding house. Pink and orange hibiscus plants flanked each side of the glass front door. It was something out of *Southern Living*.

"Dylan, this is gorgeous. You have amazing taste," she gasped as he opened her car door.

"It's not all me. I know who to hire to make me look good." Dylan winked as he grabbed her suitcase. "Come on. I have steaks on the grill and wine waiting for you out back," he said as he hurried her inside.

The interior was no less spectacular. The beach cottage was masculine, but soft. The white walls with accents in all shades of blue reminded her somewhat of her house in Tampa. A picture frame on the bright white bookshelf in the hallway caught Cassie's eye. As she lifted the sea-shell-clad frame, her mind swirled. There they were, two med school lovebirds, enjoying the beach on summer break. They were sitting on a porch swing in their swimsuits, tanned from hours in the sun, holding watermelon rinds, juice and seeds dripping from their chins. Cassie held the frame, smiling at how happy they looked.

"I found that this week in an old box in the attic. I wanted to surprise you with it. Do you remember taking that picture?"

"I remember the trip, but I don't remember taking the picture. Look at us. We're babies. And not a care in the world. Well, except for Board exams." Life had eventually become very difficult.

"Come on outside. I need to check the grill." Dylan motioned for her to follow him. Cassie could smell the barbecue smoke as she walked onto the flagstone patio. Ironically, the smoke didn't nearly take her breath away like the view before her. A bright blue infinity edge pool seemed to drop straight off into the marshland that stretched for as far as the eye could see. Large pieces of driftwood in the distance were decorated with big white birds that appeared to be standing on guard, and the marsh grass danced as the tide made its way in for the night.

"Dylan, this is gorgeous. It's perfect."

"See, I would beg to differ. That's how I would describe *my* view right now." He smiled at her, handing her a glass of chilled wine. "Any more run-ins with Rick?" Dylan quizzed firmly, changing the subject, brows furrowed.

"No. He should have gotten the separation papers today. I was glad to leave town just in case he decided to make one last plea." Cassie had finally gotten the courage earlier in the week to tell Dylan about Rick's elevator stunt. She'd known he would be worried, and that would only make matters worse. But she also didn't want to keep secrets from him.

"I think it's best if you come here on the weekends until the dust settles. That's if you don't mind the drive."

"I'm thinking I could easily get accustomed to this place." She winked. "I'm also thinking we could use an appetizer," she teased, letting her long navy blue maxi dress fall to the flagstone patio. Dylan's mouth dropped as Cassie dove half-naked, in her panties and strapless bra, into the cool blue water. His bright white smile was the first thing that caught her eye as she rose out of the water. Slipping off her red lace thong under the water, she snapped it like a rubber band at him as he neared the edge of the pool, dropping his clothes to the ground in a quick shuffle.

"Oh, you're going to pay for that," he taunted as he did a huge cannonball into the water, sending a tidal wave rushing over the side of the infinity edge.

"Gotta catch me first!" Cassie swam as fast as she could to the edge with him chasing her and grabbing ahold of the back of her bra.

"Should've taken that off too." Dylan made a swift move, grabbing her around the waist and dunking her playfully. Cassie spit water in his face as she rose up for air. "Hey, you started it, lady." Laughter echoed across the marsh as they tried to catch their breath. "I hope the neighbors don't come over to check on me. They aren't used to this much noise coming from back here. They'll get an unexpected show for sure."

Their laughter slowly dissipated as their wet lips met. Cassie's weightless body wrapped tightly around him as his hands held her close to his chest.

"I sure do love you." The words felt natural coming from her mouth, catching her by surprise. She had never imagined saying that to another man besides Rick ever again. But it felt right. And good. Cassie's shy smile and tucked chin let Dylan know that the words had slipped out without premeditated thought.

"Cassie," he said, lifting her chin up to make deliberate eye contact. "I sure do love you too." They both smiled, acknowledging their mutual feelings. "Now, let's go eat this amazing meal before it gets cold." As he carried her to the steps like a bride being swept over the threshold, Cassie caught a glimpse of something moving across the early night sky, all bright and swift like a firefly a million miles away.

"Dylan, look!" she gasped, pointing to the heavens above him. "A shooting star! Quick! Make a wish." She closed her eyes tightly and made the biggest plea for her boldest wish to come true. Her eyes popped open and with the excitement of a small child, she quizzed him. "Well? Did you make a good one?"

"I didn't have to. That one is all yours, sweetheart. Mine already came true." He kissed her softly on the cheek, placing her carefully on the stone steps like a porcelain doll. Cassie decided not to argue with him about it. She was happy to keep that star's good fortune all to herself.

CHAPTER TWENTY-FIVE

Liz

FOR THE THIRD time in two days, Liz sat anxiously on her bathroom floor, staring at the white stick. She hadn't done this in years, and when she had, she had always hoped for a plus sign. Her stomach turned as she stared at the timer on her phone. She was two days late. Since the triathlon, her periods had been irregular, but that wasn't anything unusual. Liz had never been a fan of the birth control pill. She was terrible at remembering to take them, and she swore they made her gain ten pounds of water weight. She and Rick had always used protection, except for their initial encounter in which they'd luckily escaped without any dreadful consequence. But their last meeting had been abrupt and aberrant—and unfortunately, lacking a condom.

"What the hell am I going to do if I'm pregnant with Rick's child?" she muttered to herself as she watched the timer closely. She could only imagine Cassie's rage, knowing how long she and Rick had tried to conceive. And what about John, and her boys? Her heart filled with shame. As her timer beeped, she was once again relieved at the negative result. But at-home tests are only partially reliable. She had to find out for sure. Luckily, she had quite a few connections at her disposal. Picking up her phone, she dialed the number to the hospital's laboratory.

"Natalie? Hi, It's Liz Hamilton. I need to ask a favor of

you. I need to order a pregnancy blood test for myself. Please don't let Mr. Dr. Hamilton know. It's top secret. I want to surprise him if it's positive." Liz about choked on her own words. She prayed lightning didn't strike her dead for what she was doing.

"Yes, ma'am. I'll have it waiting for you. And your secret is safe with me. How exciting!" the sincere voice reassured her.

"Oh, and Natalie, could you please push this test to the front of the line for processing? I'm on call, so I should be there in a few minutes." Liz was thankful she had that type of authority at the hospital and more importantly that John and Kelly were not the ones on call. She couldn't run the risk of them seeing her at the lab. John had taken the boys to Paul's soccer tournament, and Kelly was doing what she could to avoid being trapped one-on-one with Liz.

As Liz sat in the phlebotomy chair waiting on Natalie to draw her blood, her chest felt as tight as the tourniquet around her arm. Never in her life had she imagined herself in this sort of predicament. She promised God that if he would give her one more chance, she would never be so stupid and selfish ever again.

John

REFEREE WHISTLES AND a cheering crowd echoed behind John as he plugged his free ear, trying to hear Liz's voice on the phone.

"Liz, I can't hear you all that well. This crowd is nuts. It's a tie game. Can I call you back when we get to the car?" John yelled over the noise. He couldn't hear Liz's reply, but he hung up anyway. She got the point. Besides, he was missing the end of the game trying to keep her updated on the score.

"Let's go, Paul!" John cheered as his lanky, blond-haired son chased the soccer ball across the field. John had done the best he could to keep things as normal as possible the past few months, taking the boys to dinners and movies and wherever else they wanted to go. But spending his time with them in a rental wasn't the same. The boys were used to having him around the house to help them with their homework and hang out. He missed the couch time with them most of all. He and the boys spent most of their downtime spread out in the family room, watching sports and playing football video games. All three of them loved sports, whether they were playing or spectating.

buzz. John's phone vibrated again. Liz. After three ignores, he finally answered her relentless attempts. "Dammit, Liz! I'm trying to watch this game. I told you I would call you when it was over." He could faintly hear Liz's voice, but he could only make out about every other word between crowd chants. She was saying something about Paul being her son, too, and wanting to be there. "Liz, if you really wanted to be here, all you had to do was ask Kelly to cover for you. That's why we hired her. I have to go." Once again, he hung up trying to make himself very clear as to where his focus was. Then the texts started rolling in, which he ignored as well.

John, please don't use the boys against me. They are all I have right now. I want to know the score and how Paul did, so please have him call me when the game is over.

How desperate she sounded. Part of him had a mind to send an ugly response back, but that wouldn't be fair to Paul. Instead, he decided to ignore her like he had been. As they loaded the car full of soccer balls and smelly shin guards and cleats, high-fiving and chest bumping from a last-minute win, John heard the ping of another text coming through. With an eye roll, he tossed the phone to Paul.

"Please call your mother. She's driving me insane wanting to know the details of the game." Paul excitedly replayed the entire game to her, play by play. When the car started, Bluetooth picked up automatically so that Liz's voice echoed throughout the car. John's heart sank. There she was. His wife. The mother of his children. Her voice was different when she spoke to the boys. It was caring and tender and supportive, just like it had been with him for so many years. Hearing the voice that he loved cut deep.

"Bye, Mom. Dad will drop us off in an hour or so. Love you."

"I love you boys so much. I'll bring home some pizzas. I should be home from the hospital around eight. Be safe."

John clicked the end button on his steering wheel. The boys were quiet and so was John. In his rearview mirror, he saw Sam elbow Paul, prodding him to say something. Paul looked anxious and annoyed, but gave in to Sam's coercion, clearing his throat to speak.

"Dad?"

"Yes, Paul?"

"What's up with you and Mom? Are you coming home soon?"

John's heart sank. He admittedly had avoided the hard conversations with the boys, not out of fear, but out of uncertainty. He didn't know how the story was going to end, and he most definitely didn't want to give the boys false hope or information. He decided honesty was the best answer.

"Truthfully, I don't know. But I know for sure that your mom and I both love you very much and whatever happens with us has nothing to do with you boys." John glanced at the two blond haired miniatures of him in his rearview mirror. They both were staring out of their respective windows with solemn faces. There was more to be said.

"But do you want to come home?" Sam asked innocently.

"Buddy, this whole situation is so much more com-
plicated than you know or should know. What I want is
for life to go back to being normal again, but that's not
going to happen anytime soon. Your mom and I have a
long way to go before we can start to work on me being
back home again."

"Dad," Paul hesitated.

"What, bud?"

"Um, well, we know about Mom and Mr. Buchanon."

John's heart stopped. His vision blurred from anger.
Who would have told them? He and Liz had been in full
agreement that they were not going to share the details
of the affair. It wasn't fair to drag them through their
dirty laundry.

"Is that so? Who told you about that? Mom?" John
pried.

"No. She denied it when we asked her about it. She
blamed *you* for telling us, but we told her that we just
knew," Paul admitted.

"You guys think we're too young to notice things, but
we do. Mom started acting all weird when he'd call her
about their training stuff. She started wearing makeup to
exercise, and she was always sitting in her car talking to
him when we were at soccer practice. It seemed obvious
to us," Sam stated matter-of-factly.

John's anger grew, not at the boys, but at the fact that
he had been too blind to see what had been happening
right under his nose, yet even his children had been keen
enough to spot the affair. John was just as mad at himself
as he was Liz. He closed his eyes and swallowed hard,
trying find the right words to say. Suddenly, he heard
the loud squealing of tires and Sam's scream from the
backseat.

"Dad! Watch out!"

Liz

LIZ RACED DOWN the halls of the hospital, her heart pounding. The call had come from the emergency room physician, his words still ringing in her ears.

"Liz. It's Tom Davenport. I just got a call about an auto accident being brought into the ER. It's John and the boys. The boys are fine, but John is unconscious and is headed to surgery. I'm calling Kelly in to do the plastics. I know you're on call, but I can't let you operate on him. I'll keep you posted."

As Liz burst through the double doors to the ER, she saw Kelly and Tom standing in the hallway, waiting for the ambulance to arrive.

"Where are they? I need to see them."

"It's going to be okay. I spoke with the EMTs and the boys are stable. They're going to have a full examination just to make sure. And John..." As the words trailed out of Tom's mouth, the gurney burst through the doors, wheeling in a body covered in blood and eerily still. Liz gasped. She darted toward John, pushing aside anyone in her path.

"John! Oh God, oh God, please. Please say something," she cried as she hung on to the side of the moving gurney. The entire ER staff stopped in their tracks to see what the commotion was. Liz felt Tom grab her arm and pull her back. She yanked her arm fiercely out of his grasp.

"Liz, you're keeping him from getting help. Let us do our job," Tom said firmly.

"I want to operate on him," she growled. "Let me operate. He's my husband."

"Which is exactly why I can't let you do that. Excuse

me. I need to get scrubbed in."Tom gave Liz a sincere pat on the shoulder and breezed past her into the operating room.

Liz hardly noticed Kelly walk up beside her.

"Liz, why don't you go check on the boys? They need you. I promise I'll keep you posted on John. Trauma is my specialty. You know that," Kelly whispered gently. Liz turned to her with tears in her eyes.

"Kelly, you and I both know I've made way too many mistakes in my marriage recently. I pray I still have a chance to fix it. I trust you to take care of him." She grabbed Kelly's hand and squeezed it firmly. Kelly smiled a forgiving smile and made her way through the operating room doors. As the doors swung closed, Liz caught a glimpse of her husband lying on the operating table, hooked up to monitors and IVs. Suddenly, what she had believed was the epitome of a broken heart from Rick didn't compare to the heartbreak of possibly losing John for good. The pain was unbearable. She collapsed to the floor and sobbed, burying her head in her hands. She felt warm arms wrap around her.

"Dr. Hamilton, let me help you to the boys' room," said a sweet nurse, as she lifted Liz off the ground. Liz couldn't speak, but instead nodded and followed her down the hall, glancing back every few steps to the double doors that were the gateway to her husband.

CHAPTER TWENTY-SIX

Cassie

THE SOUND OF reggae music echoed from the band as Dylan and Cassie shucked oysters faster than the waiters could bring them to the table. The salty air coming off the ocean kept the heat and humidity of the low country seaside town tolerable. Dylan had turned into a St. Simon's tour guide that morning, showing her all his favorite local spots. An early appetizer of steamed oysters was currently on deck before dinner at eight. Cassie felt her phone buzzing in her purse, but with smelly hands, she decided it was best to just leave it to voicemail. But after three more calls, it must be something important. Cassie wiped her hands clean as best she could and grabbed her phone.

"What is it, babe?" Dylan asked as he could see the concern on Cassie's face while she listened to Sarah's voicemail. Cassie was speechless. Quickly dialing her back, she could see Dylan's curiosity piquing. She held her finger up to him, implying one more moment of his patience.

"Sarah, what happened? Are they okay?" Cassie's heart broke as she heard the news. "Okay. I'll head back as soon as I can." Cassie shot Dylan a fearful stare as she hung up.

"It's John and the boys. They were in a head-on collision coming back from a soccer tournament. They're at Tampa Regional. The boys are fine. John is still unconscious and is in surgery right now. I need to head back.

I'm so sorry."

"No way. I'm going with you." Dylan declared, signaling for the check.

"You don't have to do that. You have to work Monday. That's a long drive."

"Cassie, I promised you I had changed. You're my first priority. I'm proving this to you right this instant. My work can wait. You're too upset to be driving back alone. I can't have something happen to you. I just got you back. Besides, John is my friend too. He needs us right now."

As much as she hated for him to make such a sacrifice for her, she was so elated to see the proof. And he was right. She didn't need to go through this alone, especially since an encounter with Liz would be inevitable.

———◆———

Trying to stay within the speed limit was a challenge. A few times, Cassie accidentally left Dylan in the dust as he followed her, only to see his number pop up on her dash. "Okay, Earnhardt, Junior. Slow it down. We don't need you in the ER too," he scolded over the phone.

As they rushed into the back entrance of the hospital, Cassie was greeted with so many concerned familiar faces of nurses and doctors that already knew what her hurry was. One even had the mind to point them in the proper direction.

"Mrs. Dr. Hamilton is in B14, Dr. Buchanon."

Dylan followed closely behind her as she weaved through the corridors to a room that she had been in so many times while making rounds. Only this time, it looked different. Cassie stopped abruptly at the doorway. She could see Liz's frazzled dark hair as she sat in between Paul and Sam's hospital beds, holding their hands as they slept. Cassie took a deep breath before softly knocking on the door frame.

As Liz looked up, they locked eyes. Liz's head lowered

in shame as she saw Cassie standing there with Dylan. Liz motioned for Cassie to wait as she stood and moved to the doorway. Cassie's heart broke for her. How she could feel empathy for Liz, she wasn't sure, especially after everything that she had done. But in that moment, she was once again just Liz, her best friend, and she needed comfort and forgiveness. Placing her hand softly on Liz's shoulder, Cassie whispered, "They're going to be okay. It's *all* going to be okay." Cassie hoped Liz knew those words implied more than just John and the boys' recovery.

"Cassie, what have I done?" She sobbed quietly. "I am so, so sorry."

Cassie stared past Liz, into the hospital room where the two young blond-haired boys laid. She had rocked them as babies and spoiled them as kids. She was Aunt Cassie, the cool one who always came to their rescue when Mom and Dad were too strict. Her heart broke to think about what must've been going through their minds since John had left.

"You're lucky to have them," she whispered to Liz. "You get a second chance. Don't hold anything back. And don't mess it up."

Liz nodded in agreement, her head hanging in shame.

"Liz, your Favorite Mistake cost us our friendship and my marriage, but it also put me right where I needed to be. So, ironically, maybe it's my Favorite Mistake too." Cassie winked at her as she turned and made her way to Dylan's arms. Liz would do the right thing, she knew it. And John, despite the brutal outcome, had sacrificially gotten what he needed too: for Liz to fear life without him.

CHAPTER TWENTY-SEVEN

Liz

L IZ FELT THE gentle touch of a hand on her arm, waking her. Startled, she jumped, glancing quickly over to Paul and Sam sleeping peacefully in their hospital beds. Letting out a sigh of relief that they were okay, she sank back into the chair. She realized she must have dozed off waiting for John to get out of surgery. Liz's heart pounded, as she tried to gather her bearings. She had hoped it had all been a bad dream, but as she saw the familiar face staring sympathetically at her, it was unfortunately very real.

"Dr. Hamilton, I am so sorry."

Liz's breathing stopped. Her heart stopped. John. "What is it? Tell me. Is he okay?" she tried to keep her voice as quiet as possible so as not to wake the boys.

"Oh, Mr. Dr. Hamilton? I'm sure he's fine. I heard the ER nurses say he was in recovery. I was coming to tell you about your test results. You know, the one you wanted me to keep secret?" Natalie whispered as she gave Liz a covert look. Liz's stomach jumped into her throat.

"Of course. Yes." Liz wasn't sure she was ready to handle the results.

"They were negative. I'm sorry. I know that would have been a nice, big surprise for Mr. Dr. Hamilton." Natalie smiled softly.

"Yes, it would have been. *Very big.* You have no idea. Thank you, Natalie. I owe you. Remember, this is just between us." Liz wanted to fall to her knees in praise, thanking God for his mercy. As Natalie turned to leave, Liz scrambled to her feet, trying to make herself presentable. She had been given another chance and she wasn't waiting one second longer to start making things right. Kissing the boys softly on the cheeks, tears fell from her eyes. She had to see John immediately. As she scurried down the hall to Recovery, her feet felt like concrete blocks moving through mud. Her body couldn't move fast enough.

There he was. She could see him lying still, covered in gauze and bandages.

"Liz," she heard a voice say from behind her. "I was just about to come get you."

Liz gasped as she turned to see Kelly. "Oh, thank you, Kelly. How is he?"

"He's going to be fine. The plastics portion was the least of his concerns. He's lucky to be alive. I'm not sure how any of them survived a head-on crash," Kelly admitted. "Looks like it's going to be just me and you at the office for a while. John will need plenty of time to heal before he is ready to come back to work."

"No, Kelly. I'm the lucky one. I'm lucky they're all okay. And I'm lucky to have you here." Liz smiled at Kelly sincerely. She could tell Kelly was taken aback by her words of affirmation. Reaching her arms out, she wrapped them around Kelly, squeezing her tightly. "I promise this isn't how it's going to be. You just happened to have seen me at my worst. I promise I will make it up to you. I will make it up to everyone." Looking up at the tall blonde that she had made life a living hell for since their introduction, Liz saw in that moment yet another wink of forgiveness. Her heart leaped at Kelly's simple but profound gesture. Now, it was time to mend the wounds of the most injured victim: her husband.

Rushing to John's side, she felt a wave of relief to be

near him. As her small frame curled up beside his ban-
daged skin, she felt the warmth of his body. Lying there
on the hospital bed with him, she watched his chest rise
and fall with each breath. He was alive, and somehow,
their marriage was still hanging on by a thread too. Her
hand fell gently on his chest, feeling his heartbeat underneath.

"John," she whispered into his ear as he slept, "I love
you. I love *you*." Her voice cracked as she deliberately
emphasized the direction of her words. Her eyes were
fixed on his face as she laid beside him, thanking all the
angels and saints above that he was going to be okay.
Suddenly, she felt his hand move slowly reaching toward
her body. Quickly, she sat up. With his eyes closed and
his face still, John curled his fingers limply around hers.
Liz smiled, her heart full, knowing that she had just been
granted her third and most important sign of forgiveness.

CHAPTER TWENTY-EIGHT

Cassie

AS CASSIE LOOKED in the rearview mirror one last time, she couldn't help but be overwhelmed by a sea of emotions. Part of her wanted to shout from the rooftops, and the other part felt a stab in the heart like she had never felt before. All her nerve endings were firing and the nervous sweat running down her back reminded her of the natural human instinct to flee. But instead, she grabbed her bag and her pride and marched confidently into the attorney's office. She took one final glance at her phone, smiled at Dylan's words as they popped up on her screen, then put it on vibrate before walking into the room.

Go wrap this shit up, babe, so we can get on with our life together.

Through glass windows, she spotted Rick and his bloodsucking attorney sitting in their assigned conference room as she walked past. Cassie's expression didn't flinch as they made eye contact, but her heart pounded to the beat of her steps as she made her way to her conference room where she was greeted by her attorney, Susannah, and the mediator.

"Dr. Buchanon, you have been informed and briefed of the standard proceedings that will take place during this mediation between you and Mr. Buchanon, correct?" the mediator asked, as Cassie sat down in the modern white leather chair.

"Yes, sir, I have." She smiled at Susannah, sitting across the table. She had been nothing short of a saint. Cassie realized she was merely another client, but she felt a connection with her. Cassie had worked long and hard to have a successful career in medicine. The years of schooling and sacrifice and missed hours of sleep were totally relatable to Susannah, and the highly skilled attorney was bound and determined to keep Rick from getting not a penny more than he deserved. Rick had lost his perfect little life and he was bitter. What once appeared to be a remorseful husband, willing to do anything to gain mercy from his sins, had turned into a vengeful man, clawing and scraping for any means to inflict pain upon his victim. Unfortunately for him, Cassie had her own suit of armor in the form of Susannah and his claws were no match.

As the proceedings began, Cassie was surprised to find herself more nonchalant than she thought possible. Possessions that had once seemed so invaluable before now appeared meaningless. Susannah could sense her indifference over the negotiations.

"Cassie, what are you doing?" she whispered, holding her finger up to the mediator, signaling a pause in the proceeding. "You don't have to give in to every one of his requests. That's why I'm here, to fight back for you. I realize you're tired and exhausted from all of this, but don't let him take everything you've worked for. I don't want you to regret it later."

"I know what I'm doing. He wants what's important to him. He likes our social status. He likes his fancy car and his high-dollar wine collection. They mean nothing to me. He can have it all," Cassie confirmed, looking her firmly in the eyes. "All I want is out. I want my business, my half of our home equity and savings, and, as far as the rest of it, it's just stuff. I left all of that behind when I left that house. Besides, it's all tainted now. The diamond he gave me when he asked me to spend the rest of my life with him, he can have it. It's just a clear rock now. The gorgeous cedar chest he bought me on our first anniversary, well it's just a wooden box. The art collection that we spent so many weekends curating together as we traveled and made love and drank wine, it's all just paint on canvas. Let me take what I want and move on, *please*."

Hesitantly nodding in agreement, Susannah turned to the mediator.

"You heard the doctor. Now go get her what she wants."

As much as Rick wanted to hurt her and drag the divorce on, he loved money more. She was confident he would accept the proposition. As Cassie sat there, waiting for the mediator to return, she felt a wave of nausea. She hadn't been able to eat all morning. Her stomach was in knots from nervous jitters. She excused herself for some water and the ladies' room. Pulling her phone out of her pocket, she just needed to hear from Dylan. He would calm her down and make her feel better.

I wish you were here to help me through this. My attorney thinks I'm giving away the farm, but I just want out. I want to be with you.

Dots popped up as he crafted his response.

Cas, you are the toughest chick I know. I have your back, but you can handle this without me being there to hold your hand. Can't wait to celebrate when I get in tonight.

Cassie smiled proudly, sending him a fist emoji. She felt a little bit better after hearing from him and grabbing some water. As she made her way back into the room, she could see that the mediator had returned.

"Well, Dr. Buchanon, you have yourself a deal. Just some signatures and you're a free woman." Cassie's heart leaped out of her chest, and before she could stop herself, she hugged the mediator. They all laughed at the uncharacteristic outburst of ecstatic emotion during a divorce mediation. Cassie's hands shook as she signed the papers one by one, closing on an era of her life that she had never expected to end. As she exited the conference room, Rick was waiting in the hallway for her.

"Well, you got what you wanted," he said snidely.

"No, Rick, I didn't. What I *wanted* was a husband who would love me unconditionally until the end of time and be faithful, just as he promised. But instead, I got the next best thing, which is getting out of a counterfeit marriage."

"I'm sorry you feel that way. For what it's worth, I am sorry. And I do love you. People make mistakes."

She could see his eyes fill with tears.

"I agree. People make mistakes. Once. But a full-fledged love affair with my best friend is a character flaw. And that's something I cannot get past." And with that, she breezed past him and out the door, feeling like she had conquered the world. She was free.

———◆———

Cassie popped the cork on a brand-new bottle of wine. She'd had a feeling the day would have an epic ending. Whether it be good or bad, a glass of wine or two would be just the thing she needed to calm her nerves. Dylan still wasn't there. He had gotten stuck in five o'clock traffic. She needed to talk to someone, though. She needed Sarah.

"Hey, lady. How did it go? Are you a free woman?" Sarah's voice came bursting out of the phone. Cassie couldn't help but smile at her contagious excitement.

"It's a done deal. I never thought I would say this again, but I'm officially *single*." Hearing the words actually come from her mouth struck a chord of sadness that she wasn't expecting. A lump filled the back of her throat and her nose start to burn. She went silent, fighting back tears.

"Cas, are you okay?" Sarah's tone changed to consoling.

"Yep. I'm great," she choked out through a big gulp of wine.

"Sweetie, I know this isn't how you expected this chapter of your life to end. But I promise you, your fairytale is just beginning."

"I know that. I truly believe that. It's not about Rick as much as it is about failure. It's about admitting I was wrong about who he was and how much he loved me. It's about thinking you know someone, and you don't."

"It's okay to mourn. You have to. But don't let his mistakes define your judgment."

As Sarah continued to comfort her, she saw Dylan's truck pull into the parking lot below the balcony. She needed to get herself together. She had been so emotional lately, which was totally out of her character. She had always been pegged as stoic. But as Sarah had said, it was all a normal part of the grieving process. Cassie thanked Sarah for her words of encouragement and quickly rushed to the bathroom to freshen up her makeup, masking her outburst of emotion. As Cassie shuffled to the door after hearing his knock, she was greeted with a huge bouquet of stargazer lilies, her favorite flower.

"How in the world did you remember my favorite flower after all of these years?" she gasped, plunging her nose straight into the middle of them.

"How could I forget? I used to have to scrape pennies to buy these for you in med school. Of course, you *would* love the most expensive flower." Dylan wrapped her up so tightly, she felt like she might pop. "I am so proud of you, Cas. You are a beast." Dylan chuckled, setting a bag of sushi on the bar. "I brought dinner and a bottle of wine to celebrate."

"Oh, thanks, babe. I hope you don't mind I already opened a bottle when I got home. I needed a drink in the worst way after today. It was grueling." Cassie plopped down on the barstool as Dylan unpacked the food onto plates.

"That bad, huh?"

"Yeah, pretty much." She grabbed chopsticks and made a dive for a piece of sushi. She hadn't eaten all day. The rice was just what she needed to pad her stomach from the wine that she could already feel making her head tingle.

"Did you give away the farm?"

"Nope. Nothing that I can't do without."

Dylan grabbed his wine glass, holding it up for a toast. "To new endings and old beginnings." Cassie tapped her glass to his hesitantly, thinking he had misspoken. But as his words rolled over in her head, she realized he meant just what he had said. She nodded and smiled back at him, signaling that she understood their meaning.

Over the two opened bottles of wine, Cassie found the courage to tell him every detail that she could remember about the day. As they finally wrapped up their conversation and the eventful details and lay silently in bed, her eyes closed peacefully with her head on Dylan's chest. She just needed to be held. She was so thankful for old beginnings.

***

The churning in her stomach grew fierce, waking Cassie from a dead slumber. She jumped up and ran as fast as she could to the bathroom, praying that she would make it there in time. The expensive red wine poured from her heaving stomach, and she was reminded of how much it burned coming out this direction. It had been years since she drank enough to throw up, but yesterday's events had led to the perfect storm of anxiety, no food—except sushi, which may have not been the best call—and a full bottle of Caymus. She heard Dylan rustling around in the sheets and she prayed he wouldn't wake to see her like this. Cassie cleaned herself up as quickly as possible, catching a glimpse of herself in the mirror. Her hair was a mess, her eyes were dark, and her skin pale. Something told her this may not be just a hangover. As she made her way back to the bed quietly, no sooner had she crawled under the sheets, she felt another wave of nausea. This time, she didn't sneak past Dylan.

"Cassie? Are you okay?" Dylan asked.

"No. I'm—" she rushed off to the bathroom, slamming the door behind her, signaling for him to stay out. After ten minutes of her head being thrust into the toilet, she could hear the door open. "Go away!" she yelled, her head pounding so fiercely, her eyeballs had a heartbeat.

"Cassie," Dylan chuckled. "Don't you remember me holding your hair back on several occasions on some of our wild party nights? I have seen you worse off than this." He grabbed her curly blonde hair and a scrunchie sitting by the sink, twisting her locks into a wild, but functional messy bun, then helping her to her feet. "Come on. Go lie down. I'll grab you a wet washcloth and some ginger ale."

He was right. He had seen her pretty bad off before, but she'd been in her twenties then, and it had been socially acceptable to binge drink and puke at that time in her life. Now, as a late thirty-something professional, the stigma wasn't as forgiving.

The ginger ale and washcloth seemed to help, and she was able to go back to sleep. Normally, a good, greasy cheeseburger and some French fries would cure what was left of her condition, but when she awoke a few hours later, she was no less sick than she had been before she'd fallen asleep, and the very thought of food made it even worse. Dylan sat down beside her on the bed. She was sure she smelled like the bathroom stall of a bar on Sunday morning. Cassie tried to move away from him, but the slightest movement set her stomach off again.

"Do you think you could have food poisoning? Did

you eat anything that could have caused this?"

"Just the sushi. And we both ate it, so if it was food poisoning, you would be sick too."   She couldn't even hold water down, and her head pounded from dehydration.

"I'm not trying to call you an alcoholic or anything, but I've seen you drink way more than you did last night and not be this sick. I think you may have a stomach bug. I'm going to call Kelly and see if she will meet us at the ER and get you some IV fluids."

"I don't think I can move," she moaned. "I was nauseated yesterday at the mediation too. I just assumed it was nerves, but I guess it wasn't. Don't call Kelly. She's swamped enough as it is with Liz and John both still being out from the accident. Call Tom Davenport. His number is in my phone. He's the ER doctor that operated on John." Cassie normally wouldn't set foot in the hospital as a patient unless she was on her deathbed, but currently, she was starting to think this might be that moment. Cassie could hear Dylan explaining her condition in the next room as she slowly sat up to get dressed as best as she could.

"He's getting you a bed ready. He says you need fluids and some Phenergan, and that there is an ER full of people with the stomach flu. You probably got it from one of your patients this week. Come on, I'll help you." Dylan confirmed as he returned to the room, leaning down to help her put her shoes on. Cassie's head was spinning as she felt him lift her up to her feet. She prayed she wouldn't get sick in his truck on the way.

Thankfully, Sally the head nurse had a wheelchair waiting as Dylan's truck pulled under the carport at the hospital.

"Dr. Buchanon, you don't look so well." Sally said.

"Geez, thanks, Sally." Cassie chuckled at her raw honesty.

"We're going to get you all fixed up and feeling better," she promised as she wheeled Cassie in through the double doors. Cassie was so thankful for the IV. She could feel the cool fluids rush into her veins and the Phenergan working immediately as the nausea disappeared and her eyes got heavy. She could faintly hear Dylan thanking Tom as they caught up on John's health and recovery. Sally informed her that they were going to get some bloodwork. And that's the last thing Cassie remembered before dozing off to a drug-induced sleep.

———◆———

As her eyes batted open, Cassie sat up quickly, not initially remembering where she was. Dylan squeezed her leg for reassurance.

"Not so fast there, missy. You're going to rip out your IV." He could tell she was dazed. "It's okay. The Phenergan made you groggy." He wiped her head with a cool cloth. "You've been asleep for hours."

Immediately she was overwhelmed by the pain of her bladder about to rupture from the IV fluids. As she attempted to stand up with the IV bags in tow, Sally, the nurse, quickly jumped in to help.

"Slow down, Doc."

"Sally, my bladder is about to rupture."

"Understood, but I need a urine sample too. Dr. Davenport wants to check for any bladder or kidney issues," she ordered, handing Cassie a familiar lidded cup. She laughed at the size, knowing she could have filled a five-gallon bucket full for her if Sally requested it.

Cassie tried hard to stay awake after she finally got back in bed after the much-needed bladder relief. As Dylan repeated what information he had gotten from Dr. Davenport on John's health, her eyes batted slowly from their heaviness. She closed them, trying to still remain focused on Dylan's words. She heard him pause, causing her to open them slowly to see the reason for his delay.

"Cassie, there's no way you can work in this condition. I hope you don't mind, but I had your patients cancelled for Monday while you were asleep earlier," Dylan said meekly, insinuating from his tone that he thought he may have overstepped his boundaries.

"Honestly, I don't even know what day it is, so if you say that's how it needs to be, then I trust you, Dylan."

"Wow. I've never heard you be so nonchalant about your work schedule," Dylan said in shock. "Maybe this virus has gone to your brain," he chuckled.

"If only it was viral."

Dylan turned to see Dr. Davenport standing in the doorway, a smile planted on his face. "I had a hunch and I'm glad I went with it," he said as he made his way to shake Dylan's hand. "Cassie, you're pregnant."

Cassie's head began to spin hearing Tom's words, wondering if the meds had caused her to hallucinate. Suddenly, she was wide awake from his sobering proclamation.

"What?" Dylan laughed through his words in disbelief.

"Yes, sir. When all her bloodwork came back fine, I decided to do a quick pregnancy test to cure my hunch. Sure enough, that stick lit up like a Christmas tree in about one second. Congrats, you two." Dr. Davenport smiled at the two frozen humans as he turned to leave them alone together.

As the door closed behind him, tears welled up in Cassie's eyes, her heart bursting wide open with happiness. She smiled at Dylan as she reached down tenderly to touch her belly that held the baby she had prayed about for so long. She watched as the man she had always loved kissed her lips gently and knelt humbly beside her, burying his face in her chest and kissing her stomach. It all finally made sense: all of the pain and heartache. Life had come full circle. Cassie beamed knowing that all she ever wanted was right there within arm's reach— the man she was destined to be with in perfect time and the gift of their endurance. She couldn't help but laugh uncontrollably like a mad woman, shaking her head in disbelief.

"Cassie, are you okay? What's so funny?" Dylan asked, looking up at her confused by her reaction.

"Oh, nothing," she reassured. "Just thinking about us. And about the irony of fate."

ACKNOWLEDGEMENTS

As with any other accomplishment in my life, I want to first thank my parents, Ronnie and Karen Cole, for their love and support. Thank you for letting me reel out freely when I am certain there were times you wanted to rope me back in. To my tribe, I owe you big. If it weren't for you guys (you know who you are), I would be in a corner somewhere crying. Thank you for reading and re-reading and analyzing and cheering and doing whatever else it took to keep me as sane as possible during this process. I truly am blessed to have such devoted friends and family to lift me up. To Darrh Bryant, thanks for the amazing memories. To Alexander English, thank you for your creative energy in selecting my amazing pen name. It's perfect.

To Caroline Tolley, my plot and line editor, thank you for taking on a very unseasoned writer and helping her have the confidence to keep going. To Jessica Cave, my copyeditor, you were amazing. You took a decent manuscript and made me look like an actual writer. Thank you for your attention to detail. To Dane, my cover designer, you read my mind. To Kelli Boyd, my forever photographer, thank you for always making this chick look pretty darn good despite three kids and very tired eyes. Thank you to my staff for putting up with me on a daily basis. I'm pretty much useless without you guys.

And a huge thanks to Jennifer Jakes at The Killion Group. Hot damn is an understatement.

And finally, I am most thankful for my babies and the inspiration they give me to live out my dreams; and for God giving me the blessing of words as an outlet to heal.

ABOUT THE AUTHOR

Growing up in rural southern Kentucky, Scarlett developed a deep love and appreciation for front porch conversations. It is from these bonds and personal life experiences that she gets her writing inspiration.

Scarlett received her Bachelor of Arts degree in Biology with a Minor in Women's Studies from Transylvania University in Lexington, Kentucky, graduating cum laude. In 2005, she graduated magna cum laude from the University of Louisville with a Doctorate in Dental Medicine. She is a full-time practicing dentist in Savannah, Georgia where she has resided for 16 years.

She is most proud of her toughest job, being a mommy to three hilarious and intensely loving kids. In her minimal free time, Scarlett enjoys yoga, running, and napping. She believes profusely in indoor hammocks, firm handshakes, letting her children make their own mistakes, and that words have the power to heal.

ScarlettAdaire.com
Facebook.com/ScarlettAdaireWrites
@scarlettadaire

Made in the USA
Las Vegas, NV
02 June 2021